JAKE DOUGLAS

———————◆———————

HOOD

Complete and Unabridged

LINFORD
Leicester

First published in Great Britain in 2014 by
Robert Hale Limited
London

First Linford Edition
published 2016
by arrangement with
Robert Hale
an imprint of
The Crowood Press
Wiltshire

A catalogue record for this book is available
from the British Library.

ISBN 978–1–4448–2968–6

Published by
F. A. Thorpe (Publishing)
Anstey, Leicestershire

Set by Words & Graphics Ltd.
Anstey, Leicestershire
Printed and bound in Great Britain by
T. J. International Ltd., Padstow, Cornwall

This book is printed on acid-free paper

HOOD

When he wakes wounded in the bad-lands, he doesn't even know his own name, where he is, or how he got there. He sure doesn't know who shot him and left him to die. But when the riders come to try and finish the job, they call him 'Hood' . . . Under the scorching sun, he does the only thing he can: straps on a six-gun, gets back in the saddle, and sets out to find out who's on his trail . . .

1

Badlands

'You say my name's — 'Hood'?' the injured man asked.

'No,' answered the ranny kneeling beside him where he had propped him up against a rock, 'you said it was. Leastways, that's how I heard it. You might've said 'Good' or 'Wood', I s'pose. You were coughin' at the time.'

'Don't sound any more likely than 'Hood'.'

'Well, you'd know, pardner.'

'That's the trouble — I don't.'

The kneeling man looked at him sharply, one hand dabbing a water-moistened neckerchief on the blood-caked wound above the other's left eye.

'Don't know your own name?'

The man winced, said, 'Hey! Go easy on that cut, will you? Hurts like hell.'

'Friend, that's no cut. That groove was made by a bullet. Mebbe in ricochet at the time, but a bullet for sure. Few days old, too, I reckon. This blood is congealed but — yeah! Startin' to flow now I've softened it.'

A pain-filled right eye steadied as Hood's breathing came faster, chest heaving. Dirt-caked fingers reached out for the hand that was still working on his wound and the eye itself, the lids of which had been stuck together by blood.

'Someone — shot me?'

'That'd be my guess.'

'Why the hell would . . . ?' Blinking now that the eye was fully open again, he stiffened as he looked around. 'Christ! Where the hell am I?' The bloody-faced man almost cringed against the hot, bright sunlight. He could've been thirty or thereabouts, was unshaven, with thick, long brown hair. His range-type clothes were torn in a couple of places, red with the dirt where he lay. He was hatless, of course, squinting constantly, bewildered.

'This is the badlands, feller.'

'Where?'

'South of Hadleyville.'

'And where the hell is Hadleyville?' Hood's voice rose in irritation.

'Couple days' ride from Socorro. Them distant hills are the Manzanos . . . ' The rescuer's voice trailed off as he watched the dirty, blood-streaked face. 'Don't mean nothin' to you?'

'No more'n 'Hood' does. What's your name?'

After a hesitation the kneeling man said, 'Steven.' He was kind of a hardfaced ranny but the features softened now as he smiled — just a little — adding, 'Steven Stevens. My old man had a weird sense of humour at times.'

It didn't seem to strike Hood as very funny: obviously he was more worried about his own memory, and rightly so. 'And me? I'm just — 'Hood'?'

'Hell, pard, I dunno! You say so, I have to believe you.'

'How can you, when I dunno myself if it's . . . right?'

Steven Stevens spread his hands, pursed his lips and said quietly, 'Looks to me like you coulda been run out here, shot and mebbe chased some more, then dumped.'

'*What?*'

'Well, you got no horse, no canteen, no grub, not even a gun. I see you're half-lying on an empty holster, so mebbe there was a gun at sometime.'

'Sounds like you're saying someone left me here to die!'

'That seems like a fair summin'-up. You take that bullet-graze over your eye into consideration and I'd say it's a damn close guess as to what's happened to you. Someone thought you were a goner and just left you.'

He stopped speaking abruptly and his weathered face stiffened. Frown creases knitted his brows as he pushed back his wide-brimmed hat.

'What is it?' Hood asked anxiously. 'You've remembered somethin', haven't you?'

'We-ell, yeah. Somethin' — but I

dunno if it has anythin' to do with you.'

'Tell me! Judas, man! It's all a — a blank to me! I need to know anything at all that might help me remember.'

'Yeah, I savvy that.' Stevens spoke slowly. 'But fact is, it scares me some — you not havin' any memory and so on. Beyond anythin' I've ever come up against. Way you were mumblin' an' ravin' there before you come round, I was about ready to mount up an' run.'

'Well, do what you can, eh? I feel kinda — queer.'

'Look, my horse is pretty much jaded. He couldn't carry us both back to Hadleyville, so I'll leave you my canteen and some grub and go for help.'

'Hey! Don't do that — '

'You don't want help . . . ?' Stevens was incredulous.

'Not that! I mean don't ride off and leave me.'

'You'll be all right. I'll give you my canteen and there's a little jerky in my saddle-bags, a mite old but — '

'Christ! I'm not hungry! I just wanta get outta here! Couldn't we take turns at ridin' your horse? You know — I'll sit the saddle for a mile, then you, and — '

'And what'll you be doin' while I'm ridin'? Fallin' flat on your face soon as you try to walk.'

'Aw, c'mon! Gimme a break, will you?'

Stevens looked down, face sober. He was a tall, rangy type, his clothes marking him, possibly, as a cowpuncher. Briefly he hitched at his holstered six-gun, reminding Hood that in all ways here, the other man had the upper hand.

'I said I'll leave my canteen. *Listen*, dammit! This is what I'm gonna do, whether you like it or not.'

Hood's chapped lips tightened. 'Yeah, well you're in charge, ain't you? An' you damn well know it.' His smile widened, crooked now. 'I guess you won't leave me a gun?'

Stevens hesitated, then shook his head.

'Well, hell! What's the wildlife like here? Bound to be snakes, for sure.

6

Likely coyotes, desert wolves — '

He stopped speaking as Stevens's water bottle thudded on to the hot gritty ground beside his leg. It was followed by something wrapped in a greasy cloth.

'Last of a rabbit I shot yesterday. You know, you couldn't've been unconscious all that long. You don't seem very hungry, haven't even asked for a drink since I poured a little water into your mouth when I first found you. Mebbe you had a saddle-bag or somethin', run outta grub an' water, then started crawlin', and finally flopped. Here, I guess . . . '

Hood nodded slowly. 'You could be right. I really dunno.' He looked up at the rock-studded slope, then glanced down at his own clothes and saw the same reddish soil sticking to them. 'Reckon I could've been shot up there — and fell off the trail down the slope?'

'Possible. Pretty steep, and you'd've had to be afoot. No hoss could work its way along that narrow ledge. Look, maybe your memory's just knocked

7

slightly outta kilter by that bullet. When the shock wears off properly, you'll probably remember what happened.' Stevens was talking as he went to his weary horse, a sleek-bellied claybank, and swung aboard, the saddle creaking.

'How come you found me, anyway?' Hood asked, delaying the other's departure as long as possible.

Stevens gestured up the slope, a good way to the left. 'Was ridin' for the rimrock when I seen a few buzzards circlin' and came down to see what they were interested in. I'll be back. Or someone will.'

'Hey!' Hood grated as the other started to turn his mount. 'At least gimme a knife or somethin'!'

Stevens paused, then took the hunting knife off his trouser belt and tossed it in its worn scabbard towards Hood.

'You won't be back tonight, if at all. I'll freeze!'

Stevens frowned, started to turn the claybank, then glanced towards the west and the sun sliding down over the hills.

8

Swearing under his breath, he unstrapped his bedroll and dropped it on to the ground.

'Stretch a blanket across some rocks and crawl underneath, wrap the other around you. I'll be back soon as I can. Or someone will.'

'Yeah, sure. Either way, I'll be waitin', Or what's left of me. Right here.'

'Well, be seein' you.' Stevens squirmed a little uncomfortably and rode out into the pulsing heat haze, feeling the angry gaze of the other man boring into his back. It was real enough to make him shiver. Just once. But that was enough.

Whoever this ranny really was, he was downright scary. No! More than that, he was dangerous, even unarmed and injured as he was . . .

It was just a hunch — and a strong one — but he felt that Hood was being pursued. Whether by the law or the lawless, he didn't know — and didn't *want* to know.

He had suddenly remembered hearing about a stagecoach hold-up, just a few days ago, not far from here. The posses were still hunting the foothills of the Manzanos for the robbers. Maybe Hood had been in on it, had a falling-out with the gang, perhaps . . . or pulled the hold-up alone. Stevens didn't know any real details.

It could have been a posse bullet that clipped him over his left eye, the wound forcing him to make a run for the badlands and hide out. But he had fallen off his horse, or it had been shot from under him, and he'd somehow reached this place. Or, if he'd been part of a gang, some of the other robbers had shot him, taken his horse and left him for dead. One less to share in the loot.

It was all conjecture, dammit! Anyway, Steven Stevens had his own worries, and he didn't aim to go back and buy in to a stranger's problems. Oh, he'd tell someone in town about Hood, all right, and they could go and help, but that was as far he was willing to play the Good Samaritan.

On that thought he jammed his spurs into the claybank's flanks and set it running towards the slopes rising above the badlands.

He had put a long line of high rocks behind him when suddenly he slowed and hauled the mount to a stop as he topped-out on a rise, head cocked in a listening attitude.

Gunfire!

Coming from where he had left Hood.

With barely a moment's hesitation he raked with the spurs again and set the claybank running upslope, away from the sound of the guns as it rolled out across the badlands.

The whipcrack of rifles, the thud of pistols. Could be the posse — or the stage robbers!

No point in him riding back into a bullet. Still he hesitated. Then, *no!* He'd done what he could — and there had been a lot of guns firing: you didn't have to be a genius to figure the odds; four or five against the unarmed Hood.

There was a twinge of conscience, but he raked with the spurs and set the mount moving again.

The next time he paused to listen he heard — nothing. Just the call of homing birds, the buzz and hum of evening insects, and his mount's laboured breathing.

The guns were silent.

Whoever Hood had been, it didn't matter now, to him, or anyone else.

Except, maybe, the undertaker.

2

Sundown

Hood tightened his chapped lips as he watched Steven Stevens ride away.

Hell, that was some name to be lumbered with!

'If he was telling the truth,' he murmured aloud, frowning now as he watched Stevens spur through the first line of boulders way over there already, and disappear from sight.

He sighed, dabbed at the wound above his eye with the moistened neckerchief Stevens had left him, and gingerly felt the shallow groove that had been gouged out of his flesh. It felt like the sort of wound a bullet would make.

Now how the hell would he know that?

His stomach muscles tightened. Christ! If only he could remember! It was truly a sickening feeling not knowing who the hell you were, or what had happened to bring you to this point in your life.

He actually thought he was going to vomit as the frightening thought hit home.

Beads of sweat prickled his flesh, ran down his chest, dripped from his jaw. Breathing as if he had just run up a hill, he looked down at what he was grasping so tightly that the fingers of his right hand actually ached.

It was the knife Stevens had given him. A big one, the doubled-edged blade at least eight inches long and two inches wide, he reckoned, sliding it from the sheath.

'Could damn near double as a centurion's broadsword . . . '

He stopped breathing for a moment, turning the blade this way and that, seeing it catching the first of the sun-down fire now crawling across the bleak countryside.

Maybe his memory was going to be all right after all! How else could he remember something about Roman soldiers, something he must have learned in school, or certainly at sometime in his past.

He immediately felt better, even smiled slightly and watched the reflections from the highly polished steel blade play and dance across some of the rocks as he jiggled the knife back and forth. The light patches made strange patterns that took his attention.

He didn't realize that the play of reflected light was searingly intense enough to be seen for miles over that flat wasteland in the fast-fading, glow of sundown . . .

Not until the guns opened up and peppered his position with bullets.

He was still sitting propped up against the boulder where Stevens had set him, when the lead came whining, spitting rock chips, *zzzzziiippppping* into the coarse sand.

He rolled sideways, one arm covering his head instinctively. Grit stung his face like a handful of hot needles. He rolled, squeezed between two rocks, snatched the bedroll Stevens had left and jammed it into the space behind him. Almost at once the roll bucked and jerked as lead shredded it. He kicked off a rock, dropped into a shallow hollow and scrabbled around, looking desperately for some real cover as his vision went in and out of focus.

In the back of his seething mind all the time was the thought that these could be the very men who had marooned him here in the first place. Left him to die.

Now they were back to finish the job.

He twisted on to his back so hard that he heard his spine creak as something heavy landed behind him. He thought they might be going to start an avalanche and bury him under a couple of tons of rocks, then he realized that the thud had been caused by a man jumping down into his area.

A man with a rifle, two six-guns about his waist, a weathered hat hanging down his back by its rawhide tie-thong. The man worked the rifle lever even as his presence registered with Hood.

'You are one hard son of a bitch to kill, Hood. But I'll fix that in about two seconds.'

The man lifted the rifle and Hood, only now realizing he was still holding the unsheathed knife, drew back his hand. There was a streak of silvery light for a mere fraction of a second before the rifleman grunted, staggered back into a rock as his rifle fired.

But its barrel was angled down and the bullet geysered sand between them as the man's legs gave way and he dropped to his knees, clawing at the quivering blade protruding from his chest.

Ugly sounds came from his throat and blood spilled over his lips. His eyes rolled up under heavy eyebrows and he fell forward, smashing his head into a rock that helped turn his body so that he sprawled on his side, bleeding into the sand. Hood did not recognize him.

'You get him, Butch?'

Hood dropped to hands and knees as the voice called down from above.

'Butch? You . . . '

Hood snatched up the rifle, levering as he rolled on to his back in the confined space. The whole area was now filling with the fire of sundown: it would be dark within minutes, but they would come looking for 'Butch' before then.

'Goddammit, Butch! Will you answer me?'

Hood fired at the sound of the voice, heard a vicious ricochet, and the last part of a startled curse roared by the man above.

'Jesus! He's nailed Butch,' the man yelled. Hood could hear stones loosened by frantic boots as the man ran for cover. 'Get down on to the flat! Don't let the sonuver get away this time!'

Hood fired towards the sound of the voice and there came a yell, then a brief silence, then the loosened stones cascading down again. If he had hit the killer, it wasn't fatally.

He jammed himself tighter into the rocks as two rifles and a six-gun opened up and peppered the general area where he was. Ricochet dust stung his neck, made him wince.

He could hear larger rocks tumbling now as the others moved in. *How many . . . ?*

He should be worrying about how many shots he had left in the rifle, and on the sudden thought he heaved up and over the rock and dropped the few feet down to the sand where Butch's body lay sprawled. He bent over the man as gunfire hammered bullets all around and above him. Hood dropped flat, grabbed the dead man's six-guns, ramming one into his own belt, the other into his empty holster. He swayed dizzily.

Turning towards a closer sound, he glimpsed a shadow as a man jumped from a rock down on to a clear patch, rolled up from his shoulders to one knee, his rifle raking in an arc as it hammered at least five shots. Hood was flat on the ground by then, squirmed behind a low line of rocks, caught the muzzle flash upslope, and there was a tolerably clear line running from where he crouched up through the scattered rocks.

He didn't hesitate: he brought up the Winchester and raked three shots across the area where he had seen the muzzle flash. A man groaned sickeningly and a gun clattered as it fell.

'Goddammit!' a strained, pain-filled voice croaked. 'I'm — hit. Gimme a hand — Fr . . . '

'We don't take prisoners — nor wounded, Hal. Sorry, pard!'

'No! Wait . . . '

A shotgun thundered, almost, but not quite drowning out Hal's dying scream.

There was, of course, a big flare as the Greener fired and Hood brought up his own rifle, squeezed the trigger as he actually saw the killer, standing there under a peaked grey hat.

The hammer clicked on an empty breech.

At the same time, the man in the grey hat saw Hood, swung the smoking shotgun down towards him and fired. Hood dropped instantly, losing the rifle deliberately and palming up one of Butch's six-guns: the one he had rammed into his trousers belt.

He fanned the hammer, not worrying too much about accuracy in here, where the lead would ricochet from a dozen rocks. But he dropped flat and half-crawled under a boulder as hot buckshot screeched over the rocks where he had been crouched.

He waited for more, but the shotgun had to be reloaded, or the killer had been hit, or he had just decided to get out.

It was the last of these. As Hood strained to hear there were two different voices shouting, but he couldn't make out the words; his ears were ringing with all the gunfire resounding within his hiding-place.

He palmed up the second Colt, one in each hand now, straining to hear.

When he heard the distant but unmistakable sounds of horses' hoofs, he lowered the guns' hammers and stood up slowly.

The darkness surprised him: it was not absolute, full dark — not yet — but a heavy blanket, which gave him as much cover as it did the two fleeing killers — or maybe it was three. He thought he detected the sound of a third horse.

He climbed up on some rocks, straining to see. There was golden and ruby-red sunset fire making the bad-lands look like some unreal painting now, and he glimpsed three riders heading for the hills.

Slowly he eased down, finding his hands were shaking; he clambered on down to his original position where Stevens had helped him.

'Looks like you were right, Steven Stevens,' he said in a raspy voice. He shucked cartridges from his own gunbelt and started refilling the Colt's chambers. 'Some sons of bitches are after my hide. *Why*, I dunno. But I reckon it's safe to say they don't want to shake my hand and wish me well.'

The Colts reloaded, he sat back, getting his breath, straining now to see in the growing darkness.

He sat up straighter as his gaze fell on the stiff, unmoving legs of Butch.

He could see a tag on a short string dangling out of the man's shirt pocket, and had a sudden craving for a cigarette. He crawled towards the body, wondering what else he might find in the man's pockets.

Maybe an answer to what the hell he was doing here — apart from trying to stay alive. And why he could kill so easily.

They had called him 'Hood', so it was a good bet that that was his name.

It was a start.

Gently rubbing around the wound above his left eye, he wondered if he should be giving more thought to where it was going to end.

3

Hadleyville

He moved position during the night. In fact, only an hour after full dark he gathered the things Stevens had left, rammed the rifle into the bullet-torn bedroll together with one six-gun, and wore the other, fully loaded, in his own holster. He took the dead man's hat, although it was a shade too small, but that kept it from falling down to rub on the head wound.

Come daylight, he would need it for protection from the blazing sun that scorched these badlands.

He weaved and leaned over towards the left when he walked and warily picked his way through the boulder field, having a little light from the stars, but it was too early yet for the moon. He had gone through Butch's pockets, found five dollars and eighty-two cents, a couple of soiled kerchiefs, a deer-horn-handled pocket knife and a half-sack of Bull Durham tobacco, also a dozen 'water-proof' vestas.

There had been nothing to say who 'Butch' was.

He shucked the spare cartridges from the loops on Butch's gunbelt, dropped a few into his pockets and wrapped the rest in an old bandanna, which he stuffed into the end of the bedroll.

These tasks soon exhausted him and his left eye kept filling with blood from the bullet wound. In the end he just sat down where he'd been standing, dropping his load, stretching out and propping himself in a half-supine position, leaning back on the bedroll against a rock. His head ached. He managed to roll and light the cigarette he was sure he had needed so badly a half-hour ago.

With a tangle of thoughts rolling around in his throbbing head — none of which he could remember even seconds after they had formed — he fell asleep. Just before he dropped off he thought to ease the Colt out of his holster and hold it in his lap, careful not to cock the hammer, though he kept his thumb close to the spur.

He awoke with a start, half-rising, his load spilling, his heart thundering against his ribs. He groaned and clapped a hand to his head, which felt as if someone had split his skull with a dull axe. Although he had little in his stomach — he had no idea when he had last eaten — he threw up until he felt as if he would turn inside out. Then, gasping and exhausted, he sank to his knees, rolled sideways against his bedroll and fell into a disturbed, mumbling sleep.

He did not recognize the symptoms of concussion, but his body did; it took over and temporarily closed down; it knew better than Hood that rest was necessary for recovery. Before passing out completely he had a single coherent thought:

People were trying to kill him and he

didn't even know why, or who they were.

* * *

He woke once during the night and was sick again, but when the first grey streaks of light began to outline the slopes strewn with the myriad boulders, he felt better, though his head still ached. He swallowed several mouthfuls of the night-chilled water in the canteen and felt refreshed. He enjoyed the first cigarette of the day, although his senses swam a little after the first few draws.

He washed the wound above his eye with a freshly moistened kerchief and, with relief, found he could see quite well. He decided to take stock of what he knew.

'My name seems to be Hood. I can shoot pretty good and it didn't bother me at all to kill the *hombres* who were trying to kill me. And that's about all I know. *Dammit!*'

Not quite. It seemed he had been

mixed up with someone named Butch — now deceased — and also a man named Hal, whom he had wounded. Soon afterwards he had seen him killed in cold blood by someone named 'Fr — ' That was all Hal had managed to get out before the fatal shot. *Frank? Fred? Ferdinand? Fergus . . . ?*

He stopped the silly line of thought abruptly. There could be a lot of names that fitted and he probably wouldn't recognize the right one anyway.

But that man had cold-bloodedly shot Hal who, up until that time, apparently, had been his friend and saddlemate. What a ruthless son of a bitch!

In his head he emphasized this, felt his hands knotting into fists just recalling that callous deed.

And these were the men who were after *him*!

The sooner he got out of this neck of the woods the better.

Hardly had the thought formed before he tensed as a horse neighed not far away. Swaying, he made it to his feet and clambered warily on to a rock with a small, flat area that he could stand on, six-gun in hand.

There it was!

In his elation he even pointed, though there was no one to see the gesture but himself.

It was a sweat-streaked black, complete with saddle and bridle and reins and stirrups, well built and rider-friendly. At least he hoped so, as the animal neighed again when it saw him and came trotting in towards him.

'Come on, you beauty,' he called softly. 'What I'm gonna do with you, feller, is give you the rest of the canteen water, mount up, let you stop at the first belly-deep patch of grass and have your fill. Then I aim to give you your head and see just where you take me. Sound OK to you?'

He said this last as he let the animal nuzzle his cupped hand — empty, but which would tell the black he was among friends. He took Butch's hat, swallowed a mouthful from the canteen, then poured the water into the crown. The horse slurped thirstily, drinking it all.

'Well, hope we come to a creek or river, pard. But you take me someplace that suits, feller, and we'll be friends for life. Now, let's see if I can climb aboard and mebbe take a peek in them saddle-bags while you carry me — well, where you will, I guess!'

* * *

Despite himself, he dozed in the saddle, so the horse chose its own trail, its homing instinct taking over.

A couple of times Hood started, half-awake, but he was still too exhausted to waken fully, lulled by the gentle swaying of the black's unhurried movements.

Then came the moment when he jerked out of his half-sleep with a start that made his bones crack — briefly. He found the reins knotted about his hands and wrists and, through the rapidly clearing cobwebs clouding his thoughts, saw it was full daylight and he was surrounded by — trees.

Which meant he had well and truly cleared badlands area.

How he knew this he didn't bother to contemplate. It even slipped into his head that he was likely in the foothills of the Manzanos. A careful look around, first at the trees and then at the high-angled sun and he figured he was heading south.

What was it Steven Stevens had said? 'Hadleyville is a couple of days' ride from Socorro . . . '

Well, it looked to him like he had been riding for at least half a day, with the sun that high in the glaring sky. The horse seemed to know where it wanted to go, so he didn't try to guide it; it was an intelligent animal and picked its own way around obsacles like deadfalls and potholes as well as fallen rocks.

He had found nothing to help him in the saddle-bags; mostly spare clothes and gun-cleaning equipment, a box of spare cartridges, some jerky that almost broke his jaw, though he persevered with alternately sucking and chomping on it.

Even as the black plodded on, Hood kept looking around him, his stomach muscles tight with tension, a hand on the butt of the Colt. But there was no immediate danger, it seemed.

That would come later, and if his memory had been working properly he might not have taken over the reins and urged the horse to greater speed when the trail dropped down towards a distant town that could only be Hadleyville.

At least, he thought so: he couldn't be certain that he recognized it, though it had the look of a dozen other towns in this part of the country. *How did he know that?*

Still, instinctive caution took over, and he skirted the edge of the town, guided the horse back into some trees and reconnoitred, coming in from the opposite direction, eventually entering behind a grey-weathered livery stables.

It was well into afternoon and his stomach was growling. He felt kind of muzzy from the long half-sleep that had been with him on the ride in. The livery man came out of his office, started to smile, then the smile disappeared and he took the bridle of the weary black in one hand while he stroked its muzzle. He was a middle-aged man, looked fit with biceps stretching the material of his shirt with the rolled-back sleeves. His eyes were wary and steady as Hood dismounted.

'Grain an' feed?' he asked.

'Yeah, and curry-comb him too. He's earned some extra attention.'

The eyes softened a little and the voice was friendlier as the man said, 'This your hoss?'

'I'm ridin' him.'

'Not what I asked.'

'That's my answer, but why the question? You know the horse?'

The livery man looked suddenly on guard.

'Fact, I do know it. Belongs — *belonged*

— to a feller named Hal Banks. Only good trait the man ever had was the way he cared for this bronc. I never heard of him lettin' anyone else ride it.'

'Well, he never gave me any argument.'

Hood stared levelly at the livery man, who held the look briefly, then nodded.

'Uh-huh. Grain and curry-comb, eh?' When Hood nodded carefully the man added in a quieter voice, 'Hal ran with a kinda wild bunch. S'pose you know that, though. Frank Cooper's boys . . . ?'

'Frank lives here?' Hood tried to sound only mildly interested as he unbuckled the bedroll and two spent bullets plopped on to the sawdusted floor. He raised his gaze to the livery man's face, saw how leery the man was now.

'Er — yeah, Frank lives here, from time to time. When the law ain't chasin' him too hard.'

'No law in this town?'

'The hell there ain't! Gus Downie'll throw you in his jail — mebbe even put a bullet in you — he hears you talkin' like that.'

'But he lets Frank Cooper's bunch live here? Even when Frank's in trouble?'

'Well, it's kind of a trade-off, I guess. But I ain't here to answer your questions. Seein' as I dunno you, I'll have to ask for payment in advance. Cost you a buck-fifty-six — call it a buck-fifty. OK?'

Hood said nothing, but dug out some of the money he had found on Butch and paid it over.

'The stall'll be on top of that, you unnerstand?'

'I think maybe I'm beginning to. You know me?'

The livery man frowned, staring at the raw bullet wound above Hood's left eye, not hidden by the brim of Butch's hat pushed to the back of his head. 'No, I dunno you. But I think I seen you around.'

'There a sawbones in town?'

'Sure. Doc Hammond. Turn left at the first cross street, three houses down. That head wound looks sore.'

'It is. I'll likely pick up the horse in the morning.'

'He'll be ready.'

But the livery man was talking to Hood's back as he shouldered the bedroll, carrying the Winchester in his other hand, and went out through the big double doors.

'Sam! Sam! Get on in here,' the livery man called.

A freckle-faced boy of about thirteen or fourteen, wearing bib-and-brace overalls, came running in from the corral section, looking anxious. 'You want me, Mr Stratton?'

'Wouldn't call you if I didn't.' Stratton started to roll down his shirtsleeves. 'Give this black some grain and curry-comb him when he cools a little. Put him in that rear stall near the corrals. I'll be back soon.'

'Where'll you be if someone wants you, Mr Stratton?'

'Sheriff's office,' Stratton threw over his shoulder, buttoning his shirt cuffs as he hurried off.

4

'So, You're Back?'

Doctor Elias Hammond was a man in his late thirties, with just a few strands of silver showing in his sandy hair. He lifted the monocle he wore on a braided cord around his neck, screwed it into his right eye and leaned forward to peer more closely at Hood's wound.

'A glancing blow. You were lucky. If it had hit at just a slightly steeper angle it would've taken that part of your head right off.'

'Feels like it might've anyway,' Hood said, wincing as the clean, slim fingers probed gently at the gouge.

'No doubt you have a headache to rival the worst hangover you've ever had. But it's not too serious. I'll give you laudanum to ease the pain first, test your sight on that wall chart, then put a stitch or two in it. It'll stop the bleeding and the gut will dissolve in a few days. If it doesn't, come back, or you might feel courageous enough to tug the stitches out yourself.'

'I dunno about that, Doc.' Hood hesitated as the medic prepared his gear: metal kidney-shaped dishes and instruments clattering. 'Fact is, there's a lot I dunno about or recall.'

Hammond paused, frowning slightly, putting a few temporary creases in his otherwise smooth brow. 'You have some amnesia?'

'If it means losin' your memory, the answer's yes.'

'That's what it means.' Hammond was back with his monocle now, examining the wound more closely, pressing around it and at Hood's temple. 'Hmmm. It's not uncommon but I don't think you have much to worry about. Oh, you'll stumble and fumble with your memory for a while, like your name, for instance. But it's a good sign that you could recall that.

Your memory should clear, get back to more or less normal, but I can't tell you when or how much detail you will remember. I'll give you something else to help you sleep. Rest is an important part of recovery.'

Hood pursed his lips. 'I — er — wouldn't want to sleep too deeply, Doc.'

Their gazes locked and then the doctor nodded slightly. 'I see. Or think I do.' He raised a hand quickly as Hood started to speak. 'No! I don't want to know anything more. My patients have confidentiality but I have no wish to — be privy, shall we say, to any information you may impart — and perhaps regret doing so later.'

'Sorry, Doc. I don't mean to put you on a spot.' He squirmed and swore softly as the sutures were inserted, three of them, and his eye-socket and the front of his head began to throb. '*Judas!* That hurt more than the bullet.'

'You remember that part?'

Hood blinked — and that hurt, too.

Slowly he shook his head. 'N-no, I guess not. I don't recall hardly anything about what happened.'

'Were you in familiar surroundings when you regained consciousness . . . ?'

'I was somewhere in the badlands. Guess I'd been shot and dumped there. Or I was shot while trying to get away from whoever did it, and crawled there.'

Hammond placed a dressing and plaster over the the wound, stood back, checked the effect, then flicked his gaze to Hood's eyes, which looked expectant.

'That will hold. Try not to get it wet, and keep it clean. You certainly look as if you have experienced some — privations. You need a good hot bath to relax you and some clean clothes before you see the sheriff. Have you any money?'

'Not much. How much do I owe you?'

'I'll work something out later. I have a shirt I wear when tending my wife's garden that I think will fit you. And there's a large rain butt out in back half-full of water that lathers very well with what passes for soap out here.'

'That — that's good of you, Doc. But why? You dunno me.'

Hammond took some time before answering. 'I like to think I can judge a man . . . well, Mr Hood. In fact, I'm dabbling in a fairly new branch of medicine called 'Psychiatry'. It's to do with the study of the human mind and its relationship to a person's well-being. But I won't bother you with the details. I just have a feeling that you need help, but are reluctant to ask for it.'

'It might be that I'm reluctant to ask for it because I dunno who to call 'friend' or 'enemy'.'

'Yes. An unenviable predicament. But — '

'Hell, Doc, I'm not askin' *you* for any kinda help. Except for this.' Hood gently touched the plaster above his left eye. 'I don't want to make any trouble for you.'

'You see? I believe my judgement was correct. You do have a 'decent' streak.

Also, I have to add, I do recall you being in our town recently, and having some sort of trouble with our over-zealous lawman, Sheriff Downie. It might be wise for you to clean up here, and leave town again as soon as you feel able. Although I'd rather you stayed a little longer.'

Hood frowned, then nodded gently. 'Reckon I'll take you up on that, Doc. But I need to find out who and what I am, and what's happened and why.'

Hammond nodded slowly, going to the door. 'I understand. Now I'll show you to the water barrel and get you some other clothes while you make your ablutions.'

* * *

Hood was mighty grateful for the medic's help and consideration, but it wasn't enough. Not quite soon enough.

He had just dried himself after the enjoyable bath in the rain butt, pulled on the trousers and was buttoning the grey shirt Hammond had left for him when he heard a footstep behind him. He glanced casually over his shoulder.

But it wasn't Doctor Hammond as he expected.

It was a chunky man of about fifty in tight-fitting clothes, the pocket of the shirt sagging under the weight of a metal star with 'Sheriff' engraved on it.

And there was a cocked six-gun in the man's right hand. Some kind of memory began to stir in Hood — not a welcome one, either.

'So. You're back, you son of a bitch,' the lawman said in a deep voice, no trace of welcome in it. 'When I ran you out I told you never to come back here.'

Hood raised his hands and said quietly, 'Guess I forgot, and ain't that the truth.'

'Mebbe your memory'll improve after a couple of weeks in my cells.'

'Now, wait a minute, Sheriff.'

'That does seem rather harsh, Gus.' They both looked up to see Doctor Hammond standing there with a cup of steaming coffee in his hand, obviously meant for Hood, and smelling strongly of added whiskey. Hammond handed the cup to Hood and the sheriff tensed, his gun swinging halfway between the medic and Hood now.

'You keep your opinions to yourself, Doc,' Sheriff Downie snapped. 'You could be in trouble for helpin' this man.'

'The doc was just actin' like a human bein', Sheriff,' Hood said tightly.

The gun barrel jerked upward, twice. The lawman's face was hard, as he stepped back, watching the cup of steaming coffee warily as Hood slowly raised one hand.

'Drink that or throw it out! If it looks like comin' my way, you're dead where you stand, Hood.'

'Now, listen, Sheriff,' protested Hammond, but the lawman stepped back again so he could cover both men.

'Doc, you got a good name in this town, you're well liked, and it'd be no trouble at all to think up a few good words to put on your tombstone. But let's leave that till some other time, OK?' Downie flicked hard, slate-coloured eyes to Hood. 'You — you're comin' down to my jail with me. Step aside, Doc. This is official law business.'

Hammond stepped back, half-raising his hands.

'I need to keep an eye on that head wound, Sheriff. It could turn septic without regular cleansing, affect his sight, even. And he has a concussion which will require attention, I suspect.' Hammond glanced at Hood. 'I'll bring your bedroll and things when I come to visit.'

'You'll show 'em to me first,' snapped the lawman and Hammond nodded.

'Of course, Sheriff. Of course.'

'You better, I should never've turned him loose before.'

'Well, you've got him where you want him now, haven't you?'

The lawman gave the doctor a hard, suspicious look and nodded jerkily. 'I have. You'd best be gettin' back to your other patients, Doc. An' you get movin', Hood. See if you remember the way to my jailhouse.'

∗   ∗   ∗

Hood had been in the jail cell for no longer than half an hour when Doc Hammond came into the passageway with the surly sheriff.

'He look OK to you?' Downie snapped at the medic, obviously still antagonistic. He stood just inside the door from his front office, one hand on his six-gun, glaring at Hood, then at the medic.

'I'd like to examine that wound while I'm here, Sheriff.' Hammond gestured casually through the bars to Hood. 'I see the plaster is already coming adrift.'

'You wanna check him, do it through the bars.'

There wasn't any real argument the doctor could make about that and Hammond gestured for Hood to come closer to the bars. The doctor fumbled around at the dressing; there was nothing wrong with it but he made the examination look genuine.

'Now, it's essential that you get proper rest, Mr Hood. I dare say the sheriff can see to that?' He arched his eyebrows at the lawman, who scowled.

'I ain't no damn nursemaid.'

'No, Gus. But please unbend enough to see Hood is left undisturbed. I have the right to ask that. After all, he is a legitimate patient and I don't want to have to get any kind of legal order when it shouldn't be necessary.'

'Yeah, yeah, all right! But hurry it up. I ain't had my supper yet.'

Hammond nodded and toyed a little more with the dressing, Hood making sharp gasps of pain every so often.

'The son of a bitch is enjoyin' this!' he whispered, glancing towards the sheriff.

'Yes. He has a strong streak of sadism, our sheriff, I'd truly love to take his tonsils out some day — through his anus,' allowed the medic. 'Try to get some sleep.'

'You through?' growled Downie as the doctor turned away from the bars.

'Yes, thank you, Gus. I may look in again before I retire.'

'Leave it till the mornin', Doc. Visitin's just closed for the night.'

Hammond sighed and started for the door. 'You're the boss, Gus.'

'Damn right I am! You remember that.'

Hammond winked at Hood as he moved towards the cell-block exit door, where the sheriff stood, waiting impatiently. He paused in front of the lawman.

'He needs to keep his strength up, Gus. Would you mind if I had the diner send him some supper? I'll pay for it, of course.'

'Well, I sure won't. Yeah, OK.'

'I ain't very hungry, Doc,' Hood called through the bars.

'You'll feel much better after some hot food. I'm afraid I'll have to insist, Hood. Proper nourishment is an important part of your recovery.'

Hood spread his hands in an 'I don't really care' gesture and the medic went out, Sheriff Gus Downie scowling after him. Just before he closed the door he said to Hood, 'You break my sleep, mister, and I'll break your goddam neck. Now, that's a promise.'

'*Gracias*, Sheriff. Pleasant dreams to you, too.'

The door closed with a clang.

Then he was alone in the jail, the other two cells dark and empty. It was quiet and he wasn't quite comfortable with that; too many strange thoughts crowded into his swirling mind.

5

Loner

Hood figured he wasn't hungry but when the meal came — beef stew and dumplings — he salivated and ate it quickly. Gus Downie poked his head in, sniffing, and scowled.

'You eat better'n me, you sonuver.'

'Growin' boy, Sheriff. Er . . . why'd you run me outta town before?'

'You bein' smart?' Downie's hand dropped threateningly to his gun butt.

'No. I really don't remember things so good since — this.' He lightly touched the plaster above his eye.

Downie glared for so long that Hood thought he wasn't going to answer, then he said, eyes narrowed, 'You killed Son Loman in a gunfight, that's why.'

Hood stared back blankly. 'Who — was — Son Loman?'

The sheriff glowered again, decided Hood wasn't trying to be smart and growled: 'One of Frank Cooper's men. An' don't tell me you dunno who Frank is.'

Hood stared back, then shrugged. 'I seem to know the name.'

Downie swore. 'The hell with you!' He spun on his heel and opened the door to his office, then stepped back sharply as Doc Hammond came in.

'Thought I told you no visitin' till mornin'.'

'Just wanted to make sure Hood had eaten. I need to — '

'You need to get the hell out and come back tomorrow.'

'Well, I'm here now, Gus. Just let me check his temperature and pulse, and I'd like to give him something to make sure he keeps the food down and benefits from it.'

'*Judas priest!* God damn you, Doc. You're pushin' me.'

'Well, I'm worried about him and I thought that as I was passing on my way to see Old Buster Bacon, who's now confined to his bed with his asthma — '

'Too bad you ain't! All right! All *right*! Just hurry it up and this time, when I lock up it damn well stays that way till tomorrow.'

'Whatever you say, Gus. Mr Hood, can you step closer to the bars, please?'

The medic took Hood's temperature, examined his eyes and even his ears, gave him some vile-tasting medicine which he called *tincture of ipecacuanha*, nodding and talking to himself quietly all the time while the sheriff fumed at the office doorway.

Then suddenly Hood realized that Hammond was also talking to him. 'Hope you enjoyed that meal, because you're about to lose it.'

Hood stiffened. 'The hell . . . ?' he started.

'The *ipecac* is an emetic. You'll throw up in a minute. Sorry, but you'll — '

Hammond jumped back into the narrow passage and Gus Downie stepped aside hurriedly, his gun half-drawn, but he stopped in his tracks as Hood retched violently between the bars and out into the passage . . . several times.

'Aaaah! Christ almighty! What . . . ? Too bad you managed to step aside in time, Doc. What the hell is all this? I mean, look at my jailblock. The stink'll be through the place for hours . . . days.'

Hood was down on his knees now, stomach empty but growling and still dry-retching. He looked white and miserable, shaken.

'I'm sorry, Gus. I really am,' apologized the doctor. 'But I was afraid of this. The concussion's worse than I thought. Violent vomiting is not a good sign. Still, the next time may not be so bad, but I'll need to — '

'Next time?' shouted the lawman. 'Well, I'm tellin' you there won't be no 'next time' here in my cells. I'll chain him to a post in the stables out back and — '

'Now, you just hold your horses, Gus! And I don't mean that as a pun. This man is heading for a serious concussion and I'll need to sit up with him. But not here. I'll want to have access to my medicines and drugs.'

'Then for Chris' sake take him back to your place! If he din' look so bad I'd make him clean this up.'

'Then it's all right if I take Hood back with me to my infirmary? That's good of you, Gus.'

Downie frowned, looked mildly surprised to realize he had given the medic permission to do just that, and started to hem and haw.

'We-ell — I'm not too sure about that. I mean, he is my prisoner — '

'You haven't charged him with anything,' Hammond said quickly. 'In fact, I'm not sure why you're holding him at all. Maybe I'd better drag Lawyer Bigelow out of his poker game and have him make a ruling on this. He won't be happy, but I really do need to be close to my patient, Gus.'

'Oh, take him! Bigelow'll spit fire you disturb his damn card game.' Downie was holding a kerchief across his mouth and nose now. 'Take him. And I'm holdin' you responsible for him, Doc. He better be on hand when I come round to your infirmary come daylight.'

'I'll take full responsibility, Gus.'

'You can bet your *cojones* on that!'

'Will you unlock the door, then? I'll stop by the saloon on the way home and ask Bud Wiseman to send one of his swampers down here, shall I?'

'You do that. Aw, *shoot*! Look what I just done. New pair of boots only three days ago and I just stepped in . . . Get the hell outta here an' take this sonuver with you before he messes up my jail any more.'

* * *

Back at the doctor's infirmary Hammond gave Hood a large dose of bismuth mixture, followed shortly afterwards by a much smaller dose of some cinnamon-smelling, alcohol-based liquid.

'That tastes better,' Hood allowed hoarsely.

'Yes, it will settle things down. Sorry I had to spring that throwing-up upon you, but it was the only way I could think of to get Gus to agree to releasing you into my care. He's mighty fussy about his jail being neat and clean. Now, I've had my wife prepare some food, which you should manage to keep down without any trouble! And I've added a few tablets for you to take if the queasiness does return.'

He paused and there was reluctance in his voice as he continued: 'Your saddle-bags are packed and your horse is ready, in my back yard. I know you want to leave as soon as possible but — well, look, Hood, I'd be a lot happier if you'd stay here for a few more days so I can make sure there's no . . . relapse.'

'Doc, I — ' The medic hurriedly thrust a bowl at the suddenly white-faced Hood, then wiped his sweating face with a damp towel as he sat back gasping.

'Hood, I can't in all conscience allow you to leave without further treatment.

No! Please don't argue. I may've complicated your ailment — inadvertently, but you have to give me the chance to put it right.'

Hood was sick again, looked up slowly from where he sat on the edge of a bed, shoulders steadied by Hammond.

'Doc — you do — what you got to. I'm past carin'.'

'Well, we'll have you lying down first of all and then . . . '

Hood frowned. 'Just why are you doin' this, Doc? You'll get yourself in Dutch with Downie and mebbe Cooper.'

Hammond sobered, took a few moments to answer. 'I could say because I took my *Hippocratic oath* and I regard my profession quite seriously. Now, those things would be true but — to be honest . . . '

Hood frowned as Hammond paused and looked downright uncomfortable.

'The truth is you unknowingly did me a very great favour when you killed Son Loman.'

Hood frowned and saw that Hammond

was really embarrassed now, but the medic cleared his throat and continued: 'I'm not a violent man, Hood, and perhaps I have doubts about my own courage in . . . certain situations. But not long ago, that swine Loman had the temerity to lay his hands on my wife when she was in the back of a store, trying on some ladies 'unmentionables' as she calls them, but 'underwear' will suffice for you and me.'

He was breathing quite hard now, took a jerky turn around the room, faced Hood again, slit-eyed. 'I — I tried to have him arrested — a futile move: Loman was a friend of Gus Downie *and* Frank Cooper. No lawyer in town would attempt prosecution, and, of course, no witnesses would come forward.'

'What about the dressmaker? She must've seen . . . ?'

Hammond shook his head. 'A threat to burn down her shop sufficed to ensure she wouldn't make a complaint.' He paused, took a deep breath. 'I *desperately* wanted to challenge Loman, but I

— I — I simply do not have the courage in such situations and, well, it has been a hard pill to swallow, watching Son Loman and his cronies suddenly burst into laughter whenever my wife or I walked past them in the street.'

He was breathing harder now, long-subdued emotion ready to burst out, but he managed to retain control.

'I used to lie awake, praying for Loman to come down with some terrible illness and have to come to me for treatment. Hardly the thoughts of a serious man of medicine!'

Hood smiled crookedly. 'The son of a bitch was lucky he died quick by a bullet then, I'd say.'

Hammond flushed. 'I was badly shaken by the turn my life had suddenly taken. My wife, too, of course.' He paused, made an obvious effort to stay in control. 'I understand that you forced Loman into a gunfight because of something similar he did to one of the saloon girls.'

'He had wandering hands, all right. Ripped the girl's bodice in front of everyone. She was only a kid, and Loman was going to make her strip naked. He seemed to have everyone buffaloed, and me, not knowin' any better, I stepped in.' Hood rubbed his forehead, frowning.

'It gets a bit hazy now, Doc. But I — well, I must've put a bullet into him. Downie came and wanted to jail me, but there were enough decent men there to swear that it was a fair fight. So Downie did the next best thing and ran me outta town.'

Hood stopped talking suddenly, looked sharply at Hammond. 'Hey! I'm recallin' a few more details, Doc! Frank Cooper and a couple of his men tried to jump me in a dark alley on my way out of the livery, but I — I — got away somehow. They came after me and jumped me in my camp just before sunup a day or so later. I don't remember much . . . ' He touched the plaster above his eye. 'But next thing I knew was when this Steven Stevens found me and — well, I guess you know the rest. Glad I was able to help you out, even if I didn't know I was doin' it.'

Hammond smiled tightly and they briefly shook hands before he led Hood to a bed that had been prepared for him, probably by Mrs Hammond. Hood was glad to get into it.

'Your memory is returning remarkably well, but it does have a fair way to go yet, so I'd like you to delay leaving town.'

'Well, have to admit I do feel kinda poorly at the moment, but see how I am in a day or two. OK, Doc?'

'I'd like longer than that.' Hammond held up a hand as Hood started to argue. 'Just let me get your treatment started. You may refuse it if you wish, but I hope you won't.'

'Well, I'm feeling some better already. Is it the start of my memory comin' back, Doc?'

'I think it is. It may not happen all at once, or even seem coherent at times, but I believe you'll eventually remember and sort everything out.'

'How about you, and that sheriff, Doc? He seems like a damn mean cuss to me, and he don't like you.'

'Oh, I think I can handle him. There isn't really much he can do to me. My wife, a wonderfully charming woman with a heart of gold, by the way — Yes! Of course I'm biased! Well, I believe she sleeps easier now since you killed Son Loman; any chance I take is well worth that. Loman was an arrogant, despicable man, a bully and a lecher.'

His voice was starting to rise and he made a conscious effort to bring it down to normal level. 'Now you get some sleep and tomorrow — well, I have something that I think will help things along for you. I meant to . . . '

Doctor Hammond never finished his sentence.

The exhausted Hood was already asleep.

6

Memories — Good/Bad

The five days under Doc Hammond's care were a landmark in Hood's life.

For almost the first time he was being treated with kindness and being given expert help — and it was working!

Physically, he helped himself to a degree; it came down to what Hammond figured he could manage and the sawbones stood by to make sure he didn't overdo things. He took almost three days to fell a tree and cut it into various lengths, working his way up from the smallest to the heaviest, gradually.

He felt tired as abused muscles started to 'kickin' as Hammond termed it. He was kind of embarrassed when his appetite improved to the point where he was — with a good deal of stammering — accepting *third* helpings of Mrs Hammond's really fine cooking.

'I do believe you're putting on some weight, Mr Hood,' she said more than once, sounding quite pleased to be having more than a little to do with it.

The Hammond place was quite large, standing at the north-west edge of town, and abutted against virgin land in the foothills.

Those hills rang with the crash of pistol and rifle as Hood honed his shooting skills. He had borrowed enough money from the doctor to buy some neatsfoot oil and he rubbed it deep into his pistol holster and on the outside. He treated the saddle scabbard for the rifle in the same way.

His targets were blaze marks cut into the bark of trees and saplings at various heights, and he could be seen weaving a horse expertly between these, some-times shooting with the pistol, other times with the rifle. He also cleared a hundred-yard 'alley' and, at varying distances, starting at twenty-five yards, working through to forty, fifty, seventy and finally the full hundred, he shot at primitive targets that he had devised: a rusted coffee can (which disintegrated, it was hit so many times), the odd broken saucer or cup from Mrs Hammond's kitchen, even empty medicine bottles, big and small, and, after a while, bottle corks and his own smoked-down cigarette butts.

'My God! You are a — a walking man-of-war, aren't you?' exclaimed Hammond towards the end of day four.

'Well, Doc, the idea is to keep walkin', do whatever it takes.'

'You've had me worried, Hood. All this energy you've displayed. It was unexpected. Oh, don't get me wrong, I'm more than pleased to see it happen. I only wish I could take credit for it.'

'You can do that for sure, Doc. Without your help, I'd still be fumbling to get my Colt out of leather. What's wrong? You look kinda — worried.'

Hammond looked at him levelly and nodded briefly. 'I am, to a certain extent . . . It's plain you can look after yourself on the physical side of things, but there is still your memory. I wouldn't like you to leave with your mind all fogged in, perhaps walking into danger because you haven't recalled a hostile face or situation.'

Hood smiled thinly, took out his almost empty sack of tobacco and pushed back his hat from his forehead before rolling a cigarette.

'Been savin' something for you, Doc. Kind of a farewell present.'

'I hardly think that'll be necessary.'

Hood held up one hand as he used the other to draw his freshly rolled cigarette across his tongue. He scraped a vesta on his holster and, as he dipped the cigarette end into the flame, he looked quickly about him.

'If you're looking for Celia, she's gone to her quilting circle.'

Hood nodded, exhaling smoke. 'Just thought you might like a few more details about Son Loman.'

Hammond stiffened, his gaze sharpening. 'What can you add to what you've already told me?'

'How about this?'

Hood related, though in his own words, an account of these events.

* * *

Hood hit Hadleyville one rainy afternoon and he was broke. Not for the first time: his life alternated between eating pretty good at diners, or, occasionally some bunkhouse on a ranch where he worked for a time, and hunting down wild animals to cook over a hickory campfire.

A man not afraid of hard work, he found a job stacking lumber at the local sawmill. It was muscle-busting labour and he slept well enough on his bedroll spread in the rear of the mill's own stables.

A couple of days of this, his body aching and weary, he figured he owed himself a drink or two. There was a saloon called, simply, the Waterhole, and he went into the noise and smoke-haze of the big barroom. He tried to ignore the racket long enough to get a drink at the tight-packed bar and finally got a foaming beer in a big glass mug with a handle.

He had it up to his mouth when his arm was jostled roughly and beer spilled down his sweat-stained shirt front. He tasted blood from a split lip and swore, looked at the ranny who had crowded him: a rangy type with a flat face that made him look both comical and dangerous. The bleak gaze simply slid without interest over Hood as the ranny slapped a big hand on the bar.

'Chuck! Chuck!' he yelled at the barman. 'Where the hell's my drink?'

The hassled barkeep turned and started to curse but Hood could see his sweating face straighten as he obviously recognized the man with the flat face.

'Oh, Son! Din' see you, pard. Comin' right up!'

'I'm waitin',' growled Son and jostled his way closer to the bar while the barkeep got his drink.

'Take it easy, feller,' Hood said curtly.

'You won't die of thirst before he serves you.'

Son straightened, looked down and across his flat cheeks with those mean eyes. 'Go shuck a corncob an' sit on it, drifter.'

Hood felt the urge, the old urge that had been with him most of his life: during the Big War, Range Wars, just drifting and minding his own business, when some arrogant local son of a bitch decided to throw his weight around and start crowding him.

He set down his drink, or what was left of it, and freed his right hand. Just then the barkeep set a big fishbowl glass of beer in front of Son Loman.

'Have a big one on the house, Son, cos I missed seein' you comin' to the bar. OK?'

That got the flat-faced man's attention and he ignoreed Hood after a scathing look, and picked up his large glass. He got it up to his face and Hood felt his right arm twitch as someone yelled:

'Hey, Son! There's that li'I Pinky you had your eye on!'

That got Son's attention and he gulped half his beer, spilling much, then turned away as he set the big glass down on the bar, but it was the edge of the bar and the glass crashed to the floor. Hood leaped aside instinctively to avoid the splashes, not succeeding too well. His temper began to rise.

Son had eyes only for the small dance-hall girl called Pinky as she came out of the back room where the 'ladies of entertainment' gathered. Hood saw her mechanical smile, figured she wasn't yet twenty, and already showing signs of the wear and tear some of her older colleagues displayed. She tried to look seductive but had not yet had enough experience to be very successful. Still, she had Son's atttention.

A couple of men were making for her but Son Loman came up behind, grabbed each one by his shirt collar and effortlesly flung them aside. Hood tensed, waiting for the fists to start flying — or the bullets.

But the two rannies swallowed their anger when they saw who had put them down. They climbed to their feet and skulked away to the bar with as much dignity as they could muster, which wasn't much.

'C'm 'ere, sweetie,' Loman growled, smiling enough to show some gaps in his front teeth, and reaching for Pinky. Her smile vanished; she swiftly shook her head and started to turn away.

'No! N-not you . . . '

Hood could sense, if not see, her fear as Loman grabbed one arm, swung her back and bent to kiss her. Her head jerked as she tried to avoid him and he snarled, reached out and tore down the front of her much-laundered frilly dress. She gave a gasping scream as her small breasts were exposed.

The barroom was suddenly very quiet.

'Hey! Lookit dem!' Son Loman yelled. 'No bigger'n apples. C'mere, sis! You ain't goin' nowhere. Not till you show us all your goodies.'

She screamed louder and one of the older whores stepped forward, forcing a smile, saying something to Loman. He casually broke her nose with a fist and, as she staggered away, bubbling screams as blood oozed between her fingers, he took Pinky by the shoulders and effortlessly lifted her on to the bar. She was sobbing, terrified, and Loman reached up for the already torn dress.

'Le's see 'em, cookie! Come on, I said. Show us your goodies . . . '

As the dress began to rip down, Hood grabbed Loman's shoulder with his left hand, wrenched him around and rapidly slapped his face half a dozen times with his right, blood streaking the startled Loman's face.

'Enough! You son of a bitch!' He jerked his head at the frightened girl who had managed to break Loman's hold. 'Get outta here, girl. Now!'

She almost fell off the bar, sobbing as two other whores grabbed her and hurried her away to their back room.

Loman had steadied himself now and his eyes bulged as his rage boiled. He spread a hand against Hood's chest and sent him stumbling; drinkers were scattering in all directions now.

With his free hand Son Loman went for his gun. What most men in that bar remembered afterwards was the look of utter surprise on the bully's face as his Colt lifted into line and Hood's Colt blasted two shots so close together they sounded almost as one.

Loman thrashed wildly, went down and stayed down, legs kicking, blood spilling from his gaping mouth as he writhed and choked until he was suddenly still.

The gunfire seemed to take a long time to leave the room, and as the stunned crowd started to come to life, Sheriff Gus Downie charged in, singling out Hood.

'Leather that gun, Drifter. You're goin' to jail, an' don't be surprised if someone starts buildin' a gallows outside your cell window. Now lift 'em, you murderin' sonuver.'

* * *

Hood flicked away his cigarette and exhaled his last lungful of smoke, watching Doc Hammond absorb his story.

The medic seemed to be slightly bent forward from the hips in a listening position, as if waiting for more. Then he blinked and straightened slowly.

'So. That's how it happened. I'm pleased to know — and somewhat ashamed to admit, that Son Loman must have known exactly why he was dying — and that it — it obviously must have been painful.' He spoke the last words rapidly, shaking his head. 'I — I shouldn't admit to such feelings, Hood, but . . . '

'You got a right, Doc, if anyone has. You know Downie couldn't nail me for killing Loman, and so on. Just thought you might appreciate a few details, and that it might serve to make your mind easier about me leaving. I mean, if I can recall all those details . . . '

Hammond smiled thinly. 'I wondered just what your ulterior motive might be. Yes! You've convinced me. Your memory seems to have come back remarkably well, and I do feel easier about you leaving.' He sobered abruptly. 'Though you did have some trouble doing so before, didn't you?'

Hood nodded. 'Thanks to Frank Cooper. It was because of him and his men that I lost my memory in the first place.'

And, again in his own words, Hood continued his story.

★　★　★

At that time, Hood hadn't realized that Son Loman was one of Frank Cooper's men.

And Big Frank didn't aim to allow him to get away with the killing . . . however righteous it might be.

Downie could do nothing in the face of the crowd in the bar, none of whom had cared for Loman, but all of them had feared him.

Hood figured he had probably outstayed his welcome anyway, with Downie standing by glaring frustratedly, not to mention Cooper and his crew, so he left, went to pick up his mount at the livery, and when he rode the animal slowly through the big double doorway they were waiting for him.

He recognized Cooper's big silhouette against the lights of a store still trading across from the livery, and then other shadows crowded in. As Cooper lunged at him, Hood whipped out his Colt and laid it across the big cowman's head, crushing his hat. Frank fell and two of his men stumbled. By that time Cooper had jumped the horse forward. It whinnied and shrilled and two men yelled in terror as flailing hoofs knocked them aside, almost trampling a third man.

Hood kept going and cleared town before the stumbling, staggering men had untangled themselves.

After that, it got more deadly.

Frank Cooper and his crew raced after him as he cleared town and during that long night forced him out as far as the badlands. He hit the foothills of the Manzanos at one stage but Cooper had sent two men ahead and they triggered a volley that had Hood racing his mount, stretched out low along its back, in an effort to avoid their guns. He knew damn well they were shooting to kill.

He weaved into brush and gradually climbed higher, figuring on getting above his pursuers and maybe having a chance to pick a couple off. But Frank had out-guessed him and someone, maybe Cooper himself, was waiting, and he felt his horse going down under him even as a hammer blow above his left eye knocked him out of the saddle.

⋆　⋆　⋆

'Next thing I remember, Doc, was wakin' up with this feller Steven

Stevens I told you about working on the wound. After he'd gone some of Cooper's men made another try for me but I managed to nail one and get his gun. There's a little more to it, but you can see I made my getaway and that I'm remembering well enough.'

'That you are. You've convinced me. I will be sorry to see you go, Hood.'

'Been a pleasure knowin' you, Doc. One day I'll square away with you.'

'Nonsense. Only doing my job and I'm grateful I could help.'

'Yeah, well we'll see about squarin' away. And I'd like to find that Stevens feller, too, and thank him.'

'He ran out on you, didn't he? Left you while you were still — indisposed?'

'He *helped*, Doc, before he rode off.' Hood stopped abruptly and snapped his fingers. 'Say! I recollect you said something a while back about havin' some sort of surprise for me?'

Hammond nodded. He opened a filing cabinet drawer, took out a bulging envelope and held it out towards Hood.

Before the doctor could speak, Hood said quickly, 'Aw, now, wait up! I can't take anything more from you. Hell, I'll never be able to repay you for what you've already done.'

'This is not money, if that's what you're thinking, apart from a few dollars to see you through the first few days. Enough! No more protests, please. Look at the papers.'

Frowning, Hood tugged some of the tightly packed papers far enough out of the envelope to read some of the printing. He snapped his head up.

'What're these? Where the hell . . . ?'

'They're yours. I wondered if you'd forgotten.'

After a quick scan of the papers Hood looked up quickly again. 'Won't say I'd forgotten, just that I hadn't remembered yet. Does that make sense?'

'Strangely enough it does. You've remembered a great deal, and no one can expect total recall in one hit; it would've come back without those papers, but I just anticipated a little. As you see, you are a genuine citizen of Hadleyville — well, Hadley County, actually. Is it coming back to you now?'

'Damn! Yes, it is. I wonder how the hell it got shoved to the back of my mind — or out of it altogether?'

'You can blame Cooper's bullet for that.'

Subconsciously, Hood touched the scar above his eye, nodded slowly. 'Yeah. I've been plenty lucky, Doc, and I've you to thank for it. Now quit that! It's true and you know it. Let me tell you how I came to decide to settle in these here parts in the first place.' Hood resumed his narrative.

'I'd been on the drift with my pard, Concho, for too long. We'd been in the army together, and afterwards we couldn't settle, went down over the Rio and found some more action.'

'Like true soldiers of fortune, eh?'

'That sounds pretty good, Doc, but down in Mañana Land they preferred *El mercanarios*, mercenaries, the men who fight for money, not the Cause.

Happens to be true.'

'You weren't alone. Many, many *Americanos* did the same thing.'

Hood shrugged.

'Concho came from San Saba, Texas. His family helped pioneer that area and he had kin still living there, and a plot, waitin' for him.'

'A plot?'

'Yeah, a plot of ground in the local cemetery amongst his kin. He'd asked me long ago, if he died before me would I see to it that he was buried there.' Hood was silent for a few minutes, letting the memories come. 'I said I would — and I did. Took me a while, but I got him there. There was none of his kin left alive but the plot was reserved for him and I seen him buried decent, with a headboard.'

'That was a very fine thing to do, Hood. He must've been a good friend.'

'He was, and he'd've done the same for me if I'd died before him. Funny thing: after all them years of fighting and killing, poor old Concho never died by the gun or knife. He fell off a wagon and hit his head on a rock.' Hood paused and shook his head. 'It kinda got to me, that, and also having some place to rest for ever.' He cleared his throat, obviously embarrassed. 'Guess I'm bein' kinda stupid, a drifter like me, even thinking about some permanent restin' place.'

'It's a comforting thought, Hood. Worthwhile.'

Hood waited a long minute before he continued.

'On my way back after settling Concho I stopped at Socorro and ran into some Gov'ment man going around, askin' folk if they'd fought in the War, either side, and wanted free land to help get New Mexico settled. All you had to do was prove-up in a certain time and the land was yours.'

He gave Hammond a crooked smile and shook the envelope. 'He made it sound mighty tempting and talked me into a quarter-section, not far from here, still in Hadley County.'

'In the Manzano foothills, I think. Beaverhead Creek? According to those papers?'

With arched eyebrows, Hood said, 'Sounds right. I'm makin' progress but it's a long haul. Ran outta money and did a deal with the sawmill: that they'd pay me in lumber for whatever work I did for 'em. Which is what brought me here.' He shook the envelope again. 'You got a copy of my prove-up contract to help my memory along — right?'

'That was the idea. I'd been checking out some land for Celia and me to retire to and there was a list of people on prove-up. Remembered seeing yours among them. I take it this land is to be your final resting place?'

'Good as any, I reckon.' Hood still seemed a little embarrassed. 'Er — one last favour to ask of you, Doc. Would you — would you see to it that — I get fixed up there?'

'I'd be proud to, Hood. But let's hope that's not for a long time yet.'

'Amen to that. I figured to make my

brand an anchor. You know? Something to hold me, keep me from saddle-tramping?'

'Yes. Somewhere safe. Maybe settle down with a wife?'

Hood looked startled. 'Hell! I never thought of that.'

'No reason why it shouldn't happen. You're going back there now?'

'Yeah. Been away longer'n I meant to be.'

'Well, you seem to be doing pretty well, health-wise.' Hammond gestured to the envelope. 'And according to that progress report an acceptable cabin on the way, a little fencing started, one corral. You've worked hard.'

Hood smiled wryly as he moved his shoulders. 'Feels like it, too.'

'I wasn't certain how your memory was coming along so I drew a rough map on the back of one of those papers you're holding, but I think you'll remember all right.'

'I'll find my way there, Doc. I'm mighty obliged for all you've done, and

I'm kinda glad we'll be livin' close to each other.'

'So am I, Hood,' Doc Hammond said with feeling. 'So am I!'

7

Return to Anchor

Big Frank Cooper wasn't a man who ever forgot what he considered to be a bad turn, particularly if it had been directed at himself. He still had a scar on his left temple from where Hood had gun-whipped him the night they had tried to jump him in O'Hanlon's Alley near the stables. There was a loose molar, too, which meant a visit to the dentist soon. Even at the thought, Big Frank Cooper — six feet four and weighing in at around 200 pounds — felt himself cringe: he'd rather face a blazing gun than the clattering dental drill. He shook himself, swearing under his breath. *Dammit to hell! And Hood, too!*

He had almost squared things when he had head-shot Hood out in the badlands a few weeks ago, but the sonuver had survived somehow. Frank figured he had survived long enough.

'Too damn long,' he muttered and yelled for a man called Finn to go watch Doc Hammond's, and another man named Wilson to go and hang about the stables in case Hood hired a mount.

But his first instinct had been the right one.

Everyone knew Doc Hammond kept several horses on his small property, mostly because he was a conscientious medico; having more than one fresh horse available at all times ensured that in an emergency he could reach his patient in a hurry.

So it was Finn who came rushing in, almost out of breath, to tell Frank in his house at the north edge of town that Hood had left, riding one of Hammond's fast horses.

'When?' Cooper barked, making the highly strung Finn jump and blink. 'When did he leave, for Chris'sakes?'

''B — 'bout — half-hour back.'

'And what the hell you been doin' for that half-hour?' roared Cooper, eyes ablaze, lips tight-drawn.

Finn backed up a step or two, mighty leery of the big man. 'I — I followed him for a spell, Frank. Just to see which way — he was headed.'

'And . . . ?'

'I followed far enough to make sure he was on the trail back to his place. Then I come to tell you, Frank.'

Cooper swallowed the curse he felt rising and nodded curtly. 'Yeah — well, OK, Finn. You done not too bad.' He was strapping on his six-gun even as he spoke. 'Go tell the boys to get ready to ride, and saddle me a bronc — the buckskin. It's the fastest.'

He turned towards a cupboard, yanked the door open as Finn hurried out of the house, and grabbed a rifle. Then he went to a drawer in the table and took out a box of cartridges.

He sat down and began to thumb them one by one into the under-barrel magazine of the heavy-calibre Winchester.

If he hit Hood this time, the son of a bitch would go down — and stay down!

No one was going to gun-whip Frank Cooper and still walk around to boast about it.

No one!

*   *   *

It was full dark when Hood left town. Doc Hammond had wanted him to wait until daylight but Hood had shaken his head curtly, at the same time checking loads in his six-gun.

'I might get out without Frank Cooper knowing, Doc. Bigger lead I have the better, I figure.'

'Yes, I suppose you're right. I've had a look outside but can't see anyone watching,' said Hammond. Then added quickly: 'Not that I really thought I would. Anyone Cooper had assigned to keep an eye on this place would be sure to be well hidden. You don't have a rifle.

I have a 44.40 Winchester that someone gave me in lieu of a fee for a major operation on his wife. It's almost brand new, has only had a hundred rounds fired through it, and only about a dozen of those were mine.' He looked embarrassed. 'I appreciate fine firearms but, well, I'm no hunter. Too squeamish.'

'You? Someone who can cut up a human being, squeamish about shootin' an animal, for food or hide?'

'Take a minute and think about what you just said!' It was the first time Hood had heard Hammond speak so curtly and he saw that this was a touchy subject with the medico.

'Doc, I'm sorry. Of course there's no comparison, and — well, I'm obliged to you for offering me the weapon, and happy to accept.'

'Then I'll go get it,' Hammond said, still a mite stiffly. 'There's a saddle scabbard that comes with it and I believe I have three boxes of cartridges. I hope you won't need to use them.'

'Me too, Doc.'

Hood made his farewells about twenty minutes later. The rifle was fully loaded, there was a firm handshake from Hammond, and Mrs Hammond, a fairly plain woman but with a friendly face, thrust a brown-paper package into Hood's hands. He looked at her quizzically.

'Hold it carefully. It did my heart good to see how much you enjoyed that apple pie at last night's supper,' she told him. 'I hope you'll enjoy this one just as much.'

He thanked her warmly: he was already figuring that the pie wasn't going to last very long; he could feel his mouth watering already . . .

Less than an hour later the pie saved his life.

He was riding into the foothills, swinging away slightly from the regular trail, but following its general direction, and decided he could hold out no longer: he just had to taste Mrs

Hammond's apple pie.

She had cut it into six good-sized slices and used plenty of cinnamon and sugar on the crust — just as he liked it. He finished one slice and before he had stopped chewing, started on the second.

He had halted the horse briefly in some brush, not realizing that the leaves were sun-pale and showed his movements: blurred, but discernible.

He was sitting the saddle with one leg hooked around the horn, trying to keep steady so he wouldn't drop any of the pie: the slice was fruit-heavy and bent in the middle.

Greedy for it, he fumbled and the slice started to break apart and fall. He grabbed at it, swearing softly as he felt it squash and ooze still-warm apple filling between his fingers. He swiftly lifted them towards his mouth, head moving downwards to meet the sticky hand.

That was when the rifle fired over to his left and he heard the snapping air-whip of a bullet passing just over the nape of his neck as he bent forward.

Startled, he kept his body moving downwards, losing the rest of the pie but managing to grip the butt of the sheathed Winchester. His weight snapped the rawhide thong holding the scabbard to the saddle, so that he took the weapon and scabbard with him as he tumbled to the ground . . .

The rifle cracked in two more rapid shots. He heard one rattle through the leaves, making the horse whinny and lunge away. It was a mite too much to hope the bushwhacker would keep shooting at the sound of the running mount, but that was what happened: whoever it was hadn't seen him leave the saddle.

By this time he had flung the scabbard free of the rifle, rolled on to his belly, elbows digging into the thin layer of leaves. He swung the barrel to where he had seen the last gunflash, just in time to see another. Same place.

He had always been a good rifleman and three fast shots raked the area where the gunman was; still mounted, he figured by the high position of the muzzle flash.

There was a yell and a crash, followed by another, bigger thrashing as the man's horse lunged, likely unseating its rider. With luck the killer had been knocked out of the saddle.

Two more rifles opened up and Hood held his fire, lunging for a stirrup as his own mount swung past, trying to find an easy way out of the brush. His arm felt as if it was being yanked out of its socket but he held on, gritting his teeth, as he was dragged quickly through the bushes, spitting leaves and grit flung up by the horse's hoofs.

There was thunder in his ears but he heard voices shouting, although he couldn't savvy what they were saying.

The horse swerved and he lost his grip on the stirrup, his body rolling over and over swiftly as the animal changed direction. Then it propped its forelegs and he was flung under the heaving belly; they were in a dead end of tight growing saplings and the horse couldn't find a ready way through.

Head buzzing, he got his legs under him, lunged for the flying reins as the big snorting head shook, momentarily bewildered. He caught the leather and in seconds was settling into the saddle. Men were running their mounts towards his position now: it was made clear by all the yells and curses and the snorting of horses protesting as spurs raked cruelly.

'A hundred bucks to the man who nails him!'

That was Big Frank Cooper's voice, and there was an edge of desperation in it.

'*Cheapskate!*' Hood bawled. He triggered the rifle twice and whirled his mount in time to ram a rider coming in with his own gun up to his shoulder.

The horses hit with a thud and a series of whinnies and snorts. The other mount screamed shrilly as big yellow teeth chomped down on sweating hide.

Guns blazed in a series of wild shots. Hood lowered his head and rammed it against his mount's neck, simultaneously jabbing with his spurs.

Then he was crashing through breast-high brush and he heard the deadly swishing of low tree branches, His hat was knocked off, to hang awkwardly to one side, the chinstrap biting into his neck.

There was a confusion of shouts and guns behind him and next thing he knew the mount was plunging down a steep bank. There was a flash of something liquid, dark silver, and the sudden, thumping jar as they hit the river and he almost lost the rifle. But he managed to hold it, and still stay more or less in the saddle, half-drowned. When the horse heaved up on the far side he settled more firmly and raked again with the spurs.

They crashed through heavy brush and were in the dark shadows of trees in seconds. Weaving through the younger ones he was soon amidst the bigger trees that gave him more shelter.

Bullets ripped bark and clipped

branches, but it was random fire and the noise served only to confuse the hunters as to which direction he was travelling in.

The moon was rising when he broke out of the timber and he could still hear wild, pointless shooting as he turned away from the moon's orb as it lifted slowly over the crest of the hills.

Your hundred bucks is safe, Frank! he thought and raced on towards a trail that he remembered would bring him out on a ledge overlooking the small basin where he had his spread. Anchor . . . *Home*.

★　★　★

Big Frank's party didn't fare so well.

Two horses had been injured by collision with unseen tree stumps, one so badly it had to be shot on the spot. The other would be useless in any kind of a chase or stand-off and Cooper sent the rider home with a mouthful of vituperation ringing in his ears. That meant no pay or a chance at the hundred dollars' bounty Frank had put on Hood's head, and he'd already had the lobe of one ear clipped.

His short collar was soggy against his neck as he took out his bad mood on his mount, lashing with rein ends, gouging with spurs.

Those who stayed shifted uneasily in their saddles. Rhett Boone had a broken shoulder, he claimed, and was moaning endlessly about it. Wilson had a gash across his forehead that blinded him with blood. Cooper swore and threw up his hands.

'Christ! Talk about walkin' wounded. You goddam useless rannies! It should've been a perfect ambush but . . . Aah, the hell with it! Find your own way home. An' don't none of you come near me or I'll shoot you.'

'We — we know where he's headed anyways, Frank,' offered Alby Wilson in a voice that shook a little.

Frank's head snapped up but they couldn't see his facial expression in the darkness of the clump of trees. They didn't need to.

'Yeah! 'We know where he's goin', Frank!'' Cooper mimicked Wilson in a schoolboy's mocking tone. He spat. 'You wanta go ridin' in there now he knows we're after him? Huh? I hate the son of a bitch, but I got respect for the way he handles a gun.' He yanked his sweating mount's head round cruelly, cuffing one of its ears as it protested. 'Forget Hood for now. I'll nail him when I'm ready.'

It was weak but the best he could muster as he spurred away, heading back towards town. The others followed — not too closely.

★   ★   ★

Hood rode most of the night, doubling back twice, pleasantly surprised to find no trace of Cooper's bunch.

He had chosen a rise to build his cabin on, with well-established trees behind, climbing to the crest, where a sheer redrock wall formed a massive, natural bastion.

If Cooper — or anyone else for that matter — came after him they would have to come up the steep slope. From his position he could pick off a tribe of Comanches and sip a cup of coffee at the same time if they did.

He slept for a while among the trees and rode on just after daylight, munching on some corn muffins Mrs Hammond had packed in with his food parcel. He skirted the beginnings of the slope, in deep shadow now, and rode round to a knife-edge-thin trail he had hacked out of the brush and rock-studded ground leading up to the big rock wall.

He had survived all these years by always having an escape route ready, no matter how safe the situation appeared. The War had taught him that much — likely about the only bit of good it had done for him.

His mount was blowing by the time they reached the top of the narrow trail, the sun washing the land with pale golden light now.

And there it was! His cabin, his future home and . . . ?

He rose quickly in the stirrups, belly clenched, his heart seeming to drive up into his throat.

There was *washing* down there, on a clothes' line he had never erected! He blinked, shaded his eyes, straining to see. Yes! A man's trousers, and one shirt, a couple of dresses, two aprons, a frilly dressing-gown, all looking well worn, but *there*!

Right where they shouldn't be . . .

Even as he watched, the rear door opened and a chestnut-haired woman in a gingham dress tossed a pan of dishwater into the yard.

God almighty! Someone had moved into his half-finished cabin and made themselves right at home!

8

Squatters

There was a man working a couple of half-broke horses in the only corral he had completed.

There was too much dust and movement to give him a clear view of the wrangler, but Hood worked his way around carefully in the trees, paused to reload his guns and fix the rifle scabbard to the saddle again.

Then he eased the mount on slowly and approached the cabin from the rear, the bulk of the building shielding him from the man in the corral.

He saw that some small gardens had been recently dug and planted with seedlings, only the tiny leaves showing — but it was another sign that whoever had moved in planned on staying.

Not if he could help it!

As he approached, he saw that a little more work had been done on the cabin: a roof gutter at the rear and a downpipe leading into a battered former beer barrel he remembered getting from the saloon in exchange for a couple of hours' helping unload freight wagons.

That was when he had first heard about the railroad spur line coming down from Beaverhead, which news had made him more eager than ever to prove-up on his Anchor section.

Well, as far as he was concerned, that was still his plan; but first he would take a look at these squatters and see how tough they were, before kicking them off . . .

He had been sitting his motionless mount, looking over the small but neatly laid-out garden, the chicken coop and foundations dug for what could only be a small stable, to take the place of the weathered lean-to he had been using.

Well, they hadn't been sleeping on the job . . .

Now he heard the rear door open

quietly and he straightened, hipping fast in the saddle, his hand sweeping up the Colt from the holster.

The chestnut-haired woman who had flung out the dish of water earlier stood there with a worn-looking but still deadly carbine in her small hands, the barrel slanting towards the ground.

She gasped as his gun lined up with her chest and he said crisply: 'A gun ain't no good 'less it's pointed where you want to shoot it, ma'am.'

She coloured a little; it seemed a nice enough face, belonging to a woman in her mid- to late-twenties, he judged. Then her fairly wide mouth tightened and the carbine barrel lifted and lined up on his chest.

'You're right. I'm aiming where I want it now.'

He smiled crookedly. 'Best cock the hammer, ma'am.'

She gasped again as she looked down and one small thumb tried three times before it quit slipping off the gun-hammer spur.

'Well, you got there. But a mite slow.'
He twitched his six-gun. 'I could've killed you twice over.'

Blue eyes narrowed and the mouth tightened. 'I have my finger on the trigger, too.'

'Well, comes down to who can pull the fastest, don't it?'

She frowned and her somewhat high cheeks coloured again. 'I — I will fire if I have to. You are trespassing, you know, and I'd be quite within my rights to shoot you.'

'Believe you're right, ma'am. I sure don't want to shoot you. Just stopped to see if you'd mind if I watered my bronc and filled my canteen at your well.'

'Oh. I don't see why not.' She blinked suddenly and the carbine lifted an inch as she aimed now at his head. 'How did you know there was a well? You couldn't see it from that trail you rode in on.'

A smart one, he thought and smiled again, uncocking the Colt and sliding it back into the holster.

'I been watchin' for a spell,' he admitted. 'I heard this was a prove-up section but that the feller quit, and I wondered if I might apply to take over.'

'Oh, I see.' The rifle barrel lowered a little but not all the way. She seemed a little more at ease but was still suspicious. 'Actually, the man who was proving up died. I'm his widow, Mrs Trish Hood.'

Hood fought to keep his face blank, cleared his throat. 'I must've got it mixed up, then.' He looked past the corner of the house, leaning a little. 'I saw a man working horses in the corral.'

He let the words hang and she said slowly, 'He's my brother. My husband did not leave me very well provided for and — er — my brother had just heard about this place and applied for the transfer of the prove-up title in both our names. So, I'm afraid you're a little too late, Mr . . . ?'

He was standing in the stirrups now and said, ignoring her querying tone.

'Your brother's comin' up. In a hurry, too, almost lying along the horse's back.'

'He — he watches over me very closely. Probably has just seen you.'

Hood eased back in the saddle, his hand resting on his six-gun butt now as the rider skidded his mount around the cabin, hauling reins violently. He quit the saddle fast, allowing his momentum to carry him towards the woman.

'You all right, sis?' he panted, snatching the rifle from her and swinging quickly towards Hood, covering him. 'Just take your hand away from that gun, mister!'

Sitting stiffly erect now on his mount, Hood lifted his hand slowly out to one side, and said, 'Whatever you say. You're holdin' all the cards for the moment, Mr Steven Stevens!'

* * *

They were in the kitchen, and Hood was surprised and impressed to see that the woman was using the open fireplace for cooking. *He* sure hadn't got around to buying a stove and had figured an open fireplace would suit him, especially in the winter. But she had trimmed it up, made it more serviceable: past experience maybe.

The 'table' was a temporary affair: three eight-inch-wide rough-sawn planks laid across a couple of sawhorses. It seemed that Stevens had put most of his efforts into adding finishing touches to the cabin's exterior and the girl had done her bit on the inside.

She gave them coffee in china mugs and fussed a little over putting some biscuits — likely left over from breakfast — on a battered tin plate before them.

She seemed a little embarrassed and apologized for the way the food was presented; he figured she had probably been used to much more genteel living.

Hood munched on a biscuit, sipped some coffee, looking over the rim of the mug at Stevens. 'You didn't send anyone back for me out in the badlands.'

The girl was obviously puzzled, Stevens having given bare-as-a-baby details of his first meeting with Hood.

'I heard all the shootin' as I was ridin' away,' Steven Stevens said curtly. 'Sounded like at least half a dozen guns. When I topped out on a rise it had stopped. I figured the odds, and they came out that you must be dead, tryin' to fight off that many unarmed, wounded.'

'Had a little luck. Nailed two or three and the rest lost interest.' He raised a hand to the scar above his left eye. 'Sawbones friend of mine says you did a good job of cleaning my wound, that I might've been blinded if it had been allowed just to swell up, and the infection could've spread into my eye. So I owe you somethin'.' Hood looked squarely at Stevens, watched intently by Trish. 'But not all the work I've put into this place.'

'Your life isn't worth that much, Mr . . . Hood?' she asked, still uneasy because she was face to face with the man who was supposed to have been her husband.

She and Stevens had been caught out in their lie and now she was feeling guilty and using hostility in an effort to cover her guilt. Maybe he didn't think those exact words, but he was on the right track, and Stevens jumped in quickly: 'I did think you must be dead, Hood. I mean, if you'd been in my position . . . ?'

Hood held his gaze coldly for a few moments longer, then sighed, eased back and drank a little more coffee. 'Good coffee, ma'am. All right, Steve, I owe you for what you did for me, anyway, and I guess I'd've figured the same after all that shootin', but,' he shifted his gaze to the tense woman, 'you people are guilty of fraud and trespass.'

They looked at each other swiftly, the girl's teeth lightly biting her lower lip. Hood continued soberly:

'Didn't the Lands Commission want to see some wedding certificates? Some proof you were Mrs Hood? It's not the kind of thing they'd just take anyone's word for.'

Again he saw the touch of a blush in her cheeks.

'I told a story about a fire in the records of the church where we were supposed to've been married.'

'That'd be convenient,' he allowed. 'You improvise pretty good.'

'If you're trying to say I make a good liar . . . ' she answered hotly, but stopped when he arched his eyebrows.

'Never even thought of the word.'

She was most uncomfortable, he could see that, and suddenly she stood up and hurried back behind a curtained-off section in one rear corner: where, he surmised, she slept.

When he turned back, Stevens was looking at him bleakly.

'She's had it mighty rough, Hood,' he said in a low voice. 'Her husband turned out to be scum with some fast talk that normally wouldn't have got through to her, but, well, he was a glib bastard.

Cheat, womanizer, gambler. Gave her a helluva life.'

'He still livin'?' Hood asked quietly.

Stevens shook his head briefly. 'No. He was killed in a gunfight.' He paused. Hood kept staring hard, and Steven Stevens added, 'Yeah, with me. But she don't know that! Thinks it was someone he cheated at cards. I want it kept that way.'

Hood nodded. 'Then, you and me, we're all squared away.' He touched his scarred eyebrow. 'She won't hear what really happened from me.'

Stevens's mouth tightened and he nodded slowly. 'All right. So where does it leave us now?'

'Leaves you and your sister trespassin' and in trouble with the Lands Department for giving false information.'

Stevens sighed. 'Dammit! Look, after I figured you were dead, an' hearin' you ravin' about this prove-up place earlier in your delirium, I — well, it just seemed like it might give Trish another chance. We figured out the story that she'd been your wife and the 'burned' wedding certificate was accepted as gospel. I figured I'd be here to lend a hand and keep an eye on her.' He banged a fist down on to the edge of the plank table and coffee splashed out of the mugs. 'It seemed like a good enough idea, dammit!'

'And it was. But I'm still here. And still want to prove up so this'll be my place.'

Stevens drummed his fingers on the table edge.

'You still havin' trouble with Frank Cooper?' he asked. Hood snapped his head up and Stevens smiled thinly. 'It's common talk he's had his eye on this quarter-section, but you beat him to the prove-up contract.'

'This can never be more than a piddlin' spread, but it'll be big enough for my wants. Frank's already got a spread twenty, thirty times the size of this place. And this land doesn't even share a boundary with Cooper's place.'

'Close, though. But Frank Cooper

usually gets what he wants. He'd likely put a man in here, mebbe one of his hired guns; depends on what he has in mind.'

'That's the part I'd like to figure out. There's other land around here under prove-up. Half and full sections, bigger 'n' better. This is one of the smallest.'

'Mebbe it ain't size, it's position.'

Hood frowned and nodded briefly. 'I could go along with that, but it's no better off for water and grass; smaller areas of both than other sections, actually.'

'Then it's *where* it is.'

Hood spread his arms. 'We've got mountains, a natural stream — no diversion necessary to get water to what pastures there are. Not a lot of grass, and that limits the number of cattle you can run. Hell, I dunno. Oh yeah! And there's that bastion wall that cuts it off from the rest of the world, but it'll be a great buffer when the northers blow in winter. I can't see anything that Cooper hasn't already got, or would even want.'

Stevens shrugged. 'Well, the railroad's gonna be just on the far side of that wall. Dunno if you can make anythin' out of that?'

'The only trail around is too small for drivin' herds over . . . ' He stopped, looked sharply at Hood. 'Unless you been lucky enough to find another way? I mean, there'll be a water-tank siding. If the railroad built a few corrals they could mebbe pick up a load of cattle at the same time.' His eyes sharpened as the idea rolled around, gathering substance. 'And so get the beef to market first at Socorro.'

Stevens suddenly stood up in his growing excitement.

'With buyers bustin' to outdo each other for the first lot of beef of the season. A man could name his own price! What d'you think, Hood? Could that be it?'

'Why not? Makes sense, providing that trail over or around the bastion wall exists.'

Stevens kept staring. 'You don't happen to know of — such a trail? I mean, you been here a good while.'

'And bustin' my back to get a liveable cabin thrown up — which is first on the prove-up list. Time to worry about your herds after you get an approved roof over your head.' Hood stood up now, stretching. 'Let's quit thinkin' about it for now. Our tongues'll be runnin' away with us and we'll be throwin' in wild ideas that'll only mess up our reasoning. I do b'lieve, though, that there has to be somethin' here that Cooper wants — and badly enough to kill anyone who stands in his way.'

They heard Trish's gasp from all the way down the long room that ran the full length of the unfinished cabin.

She was standing wide-eyed just inside the doorway, at the far end, face white, hand up to her mouth. She turned her gaze to her brother.

'My God, Steven! What have we got ourselves into here?'

9

Watch and Wait

'Who the hell are those people?' demanded Frank Cooper, the anger in his voice reflected in the way he strode across the big living room in his ranch house, shoulders hunched, jaw jutting.

He stopped at the sideboy, reached for a particular bottle among a group of them and splashed light-brown liquid into a glass. He tossed it down and poured another before it had got past his tongue. He turned sharply, raking a hard stare at his four men who were standing tensely against the wall to one side of the stone fireplace. He did not offer them any drink.

'A man *and* a woman! Sounds to me like it must've been arranged before, them movin' in and helping out with the prove up. Could even be Hood's kin.'

'Think I seen the man before, Frank,' said the hardcase, Wilson, tentatively.

Frank waited a few moments. 'Is it a goddam secret?' he snapped and Wilson licked his lips, shaking his head.

'Just tryin' to recollect where, Frank. Think it was in Stratton's livery. Yeah, that's it. He was hirin' a horse, said he wanted a quiet one, that his sister wasn't a real good rider. Yeah! Now I remember: he said somethin' about movin' in to Hood's place — that he din' know when or *if* Hood would be back, but he and his sis were lookin' after it for him. Could even take over if he didn't show up.'

Frank's mean eyes narrowed and Wilson swallowed quickly. 'An' you never mentioned this?'

Wilson wished like hell he hadn't mentioned it now! Beads of sweat appeared on his narrow face. 'Well, I was gonna, Frank, but you was pushin' us to get ready to nail Hood when he showed an' — '

'Go saddle the hosses,' Cooper

barked, and Wilson blinked.

'What? All of 'em?'

Frank merely glared and Wilson nodded, kind of hunched his shoulders as if expecting a whip across his back, and hurried out.

'What we gonna do about 'em, Frank?' asked Hank Owens slowly. 'I mean, if they prove up early.'

Cooper glared. 'That ain't gonna happen, by God!'

'Who you reckon they could be, Frank?' asked Blackie Tallant, hoping it was the right question to ask.

Cooper swallowed his second large glass of brandy. 'Who? Hell knows. That's somethin we gotta find out. But I tell you this: whoever they are, if they think they're movin' in on that place, they're dead. Both of 'em.'

The men looked uncomfortable at the prospect of killing a woman in this male-dominated neck of the woods, but no one said anything.

Frank Cooper had said it all.

★ ★ ★

Hood slept outside, in the part of the lean-to still standing, and it was half-light when he woke, hand tightening its grip on his Colt, thumb already on the hammer spur.

He turned swiftly in his bedroll and unshipped the Colt from his holster as he heard the footfall behind him.

Stevens jumped and lifted his hands chest-high. 'Judas priest, man! You move *fast*.'

'And I'm still alive,' Hood added, lowering the gun hammer now.

'Yeah. Guess I shouldn't've crept up like that. Nothin' to worry about. Trish just sent me to tell you breakfast's ready.'

Hood barely hesitated; he threw the blanket completely off him and got to his feet. 'Right kind of her.'

'We-ell. Look, this is one helluva situation, Hood, We . . . we don't feel . . . right about it, and yet, far as I'm concerned, it's the best chance for Trish. How we gonna settle things?'

'Ask me when I've got a full belly.'

*   *   *

It was a fine breakfast. Bacon, eggs, cornpone fried in the bacon grease, good strong coffee — but not *too* strong, and Stevens even produced a couple of cheroots to smoke afterwards.

'Elegant breakfast, ma'am,' Hood told Trish and meant it. 'I can stand my own company, but I ain't my idea of a good cook.'

She smiled a little awkwardly, but he could see she was pleased, too. 'It seemed the least I could do, but . . . that doesn't sound *right*, somehow. I mean, we are trespassing but I'd be less than honest if I said I think we should move out and leave you to get on with your proving up.'

Hood sobered, drew on his cheroot before answering. 'I ain't gonna make a fuss about what's happened. I dunno what to do when you get right down to it, so I was wondering if we . . . just can't kinda get on with making the deadline and by that time we might've come up with an answer.'

Trish and Stevens looked at each other sharply.

'That's a pretty generous attitude, Hood,' Stevens said quietly.

'No it ain't. It's just that I got no other idea, except for me go in an' raise a little ruckus with the Land Agency, which wouldn't do you folk much good, nor anyone else, really.'

Stevens was tense now, his gaze hardening. 'No. That's a bad idea.'

'We are the ones at fault, Steven,' the girl said quietly, watching Hood's face.

'You are,' he agreed and he saw her start a little at his blunt agreement. 'But seems to me there's all good intentions behind it, not in the eyes of the law, but Steve has only your interests at heart, ma'am, and while he did leave me out there in the badlands, he'd started out to get help. It was only after he left that the shooting started.'

'Look, let's forget that,' Stevens said curtly. 'I got things all wrong, thinkin' you were dead, Hood, and — '

'You're right,' Hood interrupted. 'Let's forget how we come to this and get on with improvin' the place to the standard it's s'posed to be. Steve, I'm gonna leave you for a day or so. I don't think Cooper's gonna make any move against you yet awhile, 'specially if I'm not around.'

Stevens frowned. 'Nothin's changed, Hood. Whether you're around or not, Cooper's still gonna want this place.'

'Yeah, I agree. But I've got to see someone, and if I'm right about this thing we'll have cause to celebrate. We might still have Cooper to contend with, but we'll have the Gov'ment on our side and he'll have to pull his horns in pronto.'

Trish had been studying him intently and now she smiled slowly. 'All on account of you liked your breakfast?'

'No, on account of I see a way for us all to prosper and get Cooper off our

backs at the same time. You folk willin'
to stay and trust me while I go back to
Hadleyville and see to it?'

Trish and Stevens looked at each
other. Both smiled as Hood rose to his
feet.

'That's what I figured,' he said.

★   ★   ★

As he swung aboard his buckskin and
settled in the saddle Stevens came round
the corner of the cabin from where the
tools were kept. He was carrying an axe
and a couple of cold chisels; a hammer
was stuck through his belt.

'I think I seen someone.' He lifted the
hand holding the axe and casually
pointed with the blade as he let it sag
towards the ground. 'Sittin' a paint
pony, which was how I spotted him, the
colour stickin' out among the greenery.'

'Feller named Wilson forks a paint.
Cooper's wrangler.'

'Think he's still there. He'll report to
Frank when you ride out, I guess.'

Hood lifted the reins. 'Might even trail me for a little, see where I'm goin'.'

'You don't sound worried.'

'Mebbe I can have a little talk with him. You stay close to the cabin and keep an' eye on Trish.'

Stevens nodded, but he was frowning, obviously worried.

★   ★   ★

Hood did some fast riding, weaving between thick timber and fields of boulders. He smiled to himself as he crouched behind a big round rock and watched Wilson skidding his mount this way and that, trying to make out the deliberate tangle of tracks Hood had left.

He waited as Wilson gradually drew closer, swearing aloud, taking out his bad mood on his mount and thereby making it even harder to catch up with Hood.

So Hood made it easy for him, working around slowly until, when he turned at the northside edge of the big rock, he was behind Wilson.

'This way, Wilson.'

Frank Cooper's man jerked in the saddle. Hood swore later that he actually saw the blood drain out of Wilson's startled face. But only for a moment. He was a hardcase, no matter how many brains he had — or lacked — and he jumped his paint pony aside, drawing his Winchester awkwardly from the saddle scabbard.

'You damn fool,' Hood said with a brief, disparaging laugh. He held his cocked six-gun on the other man. 'You'll be here till next Sunday week getting that full-length rifle outta that scabbard. You could've been gettin' off your second or third shot by now if you'd gone for your Colt.'

'That — so?' Wilson said, the words partly distorted by a cough in the back of his throat. But he surprised Hood by swinging up the Winchester, and Hood saw that he had been mistaken: the gun was a carbine, with a much shorter barrel than the rifle he had figured it

126

for, but the scabbard was for a full-size rifle.

Wilson triggered and it was wild, perhaps on purpose, just to divert Hood. But Hood swayed in the saddle, came forward with a jolt on to his claybank's neck and yelled in its ear, at the same time ramming home his heels.

The horse gave a snort and shot like an arrow into Wilson's mount. The jolt unseated both men and Wilson lost the carbine, aided by a sweeping blow from Hood's pistol. The barrels clanked as metal struck metal and Wilson's eyes widened as he felt his mount going down under him. He kicked his boots free of the stirrups and tried to swing his left leg over the saddle horn. But Hood's claybank was ramming forward still, practically climbing on to the paint's back, jamming the now wildly yelling Wilson.

They hit in a thrashing that stirred up a miniature dust storm. Hood leaned down from the whinnying claybank and swung his Colt against

Wilson's head, hard enough to send the man's hat flying. The hard case himself soon followed it into the dust, twisted and rolled and kicked frantically to keep away from the trampling hoofs.

Hood had control of his mount; he freed a boot from the stirrup and drove it into the side of Wilson's head.

The man's feet left the ground and he collapsed in a huddle, covered in dust and grit from the mêlée, face bloody and head ringing like the Angelus in a Spanish cathedral at eventide.

He came round, feeling the weight of Hood's boot across his throat. His eyes bulged as Hood leaned into him a little more. He grabbed at the dusty, scuffed leather, unable to shift it, making frantic gargling sounds.

Hood eased back slightly. 'We gonna talk a little. OK?'

Wilson nodded desperately, the sounds becoming harsh as he scrabbled at the boot. Hood didn't let up the pressure right away.

'I mean it, Wilson. We talk and you

tell me what I want to know or you'll die from a crushed larynx.' He shook his head and pursed his lips. 'Seen a couple men die that way in the War; real ugly, thrashin', coughing blood, face the colour of beetroot; one feller even bit clear through . . . Aw, OK, you got the idea, I see.'

He eased up the pressure and Wilson grasped his bruised and dirty throat, air whistling and rasping as he sucked it down into his lungs.

Hood squatted beside him, watching, then placed his Colt's barrel against Wilson's right ear. 'Now, if I shoot, you lose an ear and you'll be deaf for the rest of your life, which I reckon won't be for too long once Cooper gets the word that you spilled your guts to me.'

Wilson's reddened eyes filled with tears as he shook his head wildly.

Hood went on: 'Frank's a real mean son of a bitch, huh? S'pose he has to be, runnin' a bunch of stupid, sadistic scum like you and your pards. You agree? Hey, that was quick! Wise man, though. OK. I'm gonna ask you a coupla questions and you're gonna answer 'em — truthfully. Right?'

Hood thought the terrified man's head might snap his neck, he kept nodding agreement so violently and for so long.

* * *

Doc Hammond looked surprised when he opened his side door and found Hood standing on the top step.

'Well. Must say I wasn't expecting a return visit from you so soon. Best come in and let me look at that graze on your cheek.' The medic stepped aside and frowned as Hood entered. 'Though I must say, it does look rather minor . . .'

Hood touched the fresh graze lightly as they sat down in the small office, crowded with a desk, a couple of cupboards and a small table where Hood figured the medic did minor operations. Hood hadn't been in here before, and as he looked around, he said: 'Forget the graze, Doc, that's not why I'm here.' He turned to Hammond, who was behind his desk. 'What're those old framed drawings on the wall, Doc? They look like maps.'

Hammond barely glanced at the three framed items Hood indicated. 'Yes, old maps from the days of the Conquistadors. I happen to like their embellishments of clouds and the angelic faces of cherubs blowing imaginary ships across an imaginary sea.' He paused, face somewhat changed with a rising embarrassment. 'Reminds me of illustrations in old seafaring books my grandfather used to read to me while I sat on his knee. These only show some of the country around here, not hidden treasure as I liked to imagine in the maps I pored over in my boyhood. I must've copied dozens from books, practically papered the walls of my room, much to my mother's ire.'

'Are these real?'

'Oh, yes. Well, based on real old

maps, touched up here and there to make them presentable. Two are copies, the third *is* an original that I tracked down some years ago, so I framed it. I think they make good decorations.'

'Yeah, they do. Look, Doc, you know in general about the folk I've got living on my quarter-section, don't you?' As Hammond nodded, obviously puzzled, Hood told him what he knew about Trish and Steven Stevens.

'Steve had good reason to think I was dead and he saw a chance to help out his sister after the rough life she'd led. I have no real hassle with them doing what they did. But they could be in a lot of trouble with the Lands Department, seeing as I've come back to life so to speak.'

'Yes, I can see that, and the fact you were supposed to be *married* to the lady?'

'Doc, they're good people. I'm not sayin' I'm happy with the situation, and it might take some workin'-out later, but I don't want to see 'em in any real trouble.'

'No. It could mean jail, certainly for the man, and the lady's life would be more or less ruined, I should think, for misleading the Lands Department as they did.'

'Yeah. That's what bothers me. I've come up with a kinda answer to it, but I'll need you to back me up.'

Hammond was studying Hood's face carefully. 'In what way?'

Hood sighed and made a kind of helpless gesture with his hands. 'Well, if you'll go along with me when I tell the land agent I really did lose my memory.'

'Of course. You *did* have transient amnesia and I wouldn't hesitate to endorse that claim.'

'Thanks, Doc. You see, I can say I forgot that I had a wife, temporarily, but now that she's kind of inherited the quarter-section, that's OK with me.'

'I see. That'd make it perfectly legal, no subterfuge perpetrated, nor intended,' observed the medic. 'Yes, of course I'll go along with that part, Hood, but *is* there a real marriage?' Hood shook his head, watching Hammond closely.

But the doctor merely nodded. 'Well, as I told you once, I like to think I can judge people and their actions pretty well, and I'm fairly sure you can make your own judgements with a good deal of accuracy.'

Hood released a long breath. 'Thanks, Doc. I — I owe Stevens for what he did for me before he rode out and heard the shooting that he'd thought had finished me.'

'That's mighty generous of you, Hood. And you'd like me to accompany you to the Land Agency while you make your explanations, I suppose. Is that it?'

'It is. I don't expect you to lie for me, Doc, just confirm that I did have amnesia for a while.'

'I'll write an affidavit, backing your amnesia story. I'm sure Agent McGill will accept it. Although I may have to make the declaration before a lawyer.'

'Much obliged, Doc.'

'Er, I feel I have to say that I'm not at all certain this will diminish Frank

Cooper's interest in your land in any way.'

'No, guess not, but that part's for me to handle.'

The doctor had gone to a cabinet and now brought out paper and other writing materials. As he sat down at the small desk, arranging them, he glanced up at Hood.

'I know Frank Cooper is one man I have judged correctly. He's a bully, and his honesty has been questioned more than once, though it's never been proved that he does act outside the law; but his greed will be his downfall.'

Hood let Hammond write a few lines before saying, 'Stevens and I kinda worked out why Cooper's after my land, Doc. I guess you could call it plain greed.' He swiftly explained the theory he and Stevens had come up with, about finding a short cut over, around or even through the big rock wall, so as to have first call on beef prices as far west as Socorro.

Hammond suddenly stood up, walked

to the genuine Spanish map and tapped the frame. 'Come here and I'll show you something that might interest you, Hood.' He tapped a lower shaded section of the series of criss-crossing thick and thin lines. 'That shaded area is the bastion wall. Bend closer and you'll see the old Spanish words still legible on the original chart. First *Muralia*, and here, *Muro*. Now look at that thick but faded curving line.'

Hood squinted, leaned closer, touched the lines.

His mouth was suddenly dry.

'This one? Seems to go around the end of the wall or — hell! Hard to make out, Doc. Almost looks as if it goes *into* the wall. But that can't be right.'

'I agree it's difficult to make out just where it lies in relation to the wall, but it's on your quarter-section, whatever it is.'

Hammond indicated some longitudinal notations along the map's edges, almost hidden by the frame.

'Yeah, I can see that, but what is it?'

The doctor smiled. 'Someone who ought to know once told me that as far as he was concerned it was proof that the so-called 'back door' to the badlands actually existed, and was used by the Spanish to escape marauding Indians and even posses of *Americano* settlers, before Spain relinquished New Mexico. Those early pioneers used to drive their cattle over that trail, through to what were grassy plains at that time. Though they've deteriorated somewhat these days.'

Hammond smiled as he saw the growing realization on Hood's face.

'Yes, Hood. Quite possibly it is the fabled trail that has now all but disappeared beneath a hundred years or more of landslides and washaways, and all on your land.'

10

'L' as in 'Law'

Land Agent Lucas McGill was a stern-faced forty-eight-year-old with receding brown hair that was becoming liberally sprinkled with grey. He had a habit of sniffing quite noticeably before speaking and he did this now as he glanced up from the affidavit Doctor Hammond had handed him. McGill looked from the medic to Hood standing beside him and tapped the paper he held.

'Nicely worded, Doctor, and very much to the point. It will stand up in any court of law, I expect. Providing it is declared and witnessed before a properly gazetted lawyer. Sullivan would be an excellent choice. But feel free to see someone else if you wish.'

'Yes, I rather thought a lawyer might have to be consulted. Harley Sullivan is

138

quite acceptable, Lucas.'

Hammond took the paper and folded it before putting it in his jacket pocket.

'I'll go and attend to that, Hood, while you complete your own businesss here.'

The doctor nodded and left the Land Agency by the front door. McGill looked up at Hood.

'I presume you wish me to accept your . . . wife's and her brother's claim to take over the prove-up conditions as they had applied for, on its merits?'

'I'd sure appreciate that, Mr McGill.' Hood gave an on-off smile. 'I ain't used to being so . . . forgetful.' He touched the scar above his left eye by way of emphasis.

'To forget one had a wife? Even if only temporarily?' For a moment Agent McGill looked almost wistful, but then he cleared his throat and shuffled some papers before him. He sniffed hard. 'Yes, well, when the good doctor brings back his witnessed affidavit I see no reason why whatever arrangement you wish to make with Mrs Hood and her brother can't go ahead, quite legally. I am responsible for the settling and distribution of the land here, but I like to think that the 'L' in 'Land' also stands for 'Law', as a capital letter, of course.'

He paused and Hood nodded quickly, figuring he was meant to show both his attention and appreciation.

'Er, I have heard a whisper that there is some dissension between you and a rancher named Frank Cooper.' McGill didn't wait for Hood to confirm or deny, but continued: 'Mr Cooper has a reputation for bullying, riding roughshod over people he considers to be blocking his desires, and generally acting downright illegally. He appears to have got away with such behaviour many times in the past but this will not be the case here.'

'Glad to hear it. I . . . '

McGill lifted a hand, adding: 'Any arguments over this land, which, I hear, you are calling 'Anchorage'?'

''Anchor',' Hood corrected, and

McGill made a note or a correction on the papers before him.

'Any arguments, as I said, will be referred to me and decided by me. Is that clear?'

'Sure, that's fine.'

McGill gave him a sharp look. 'Well, I appreciate your concurrence, Hood.' There was heavy irony in his tone and Hood quickly settled himself in an attentive attitude.

'You see, something Mr Cooper may have overlooked is that this is still Federal land, until such time as what we call 'the parcel', meaning the designated area, is proved up to our accepted levels. So, *if* there is any form of violence or interference with our settlers carrying out their legal obligations, I will not hesitate to send for a United States Marshal.'

That surprised Hood, but it was a good kind of surprise. He started to comment but McGill's hand waved again, giving him pause.

'I will be posting a public notice to

that effect by this afternoon. All ranchers and settlers will be advised, or perhaps you would care to pass along this information to Mr Frank Cooper in person?'

'Oh, I reckon I'd like that!'

Again the cautionary hand flapped. 'On second thoughts, perhaps no. It is my responsibility and I should see to it personally.' McGill almost smiled, adding: 'And it would be in no one's best interests if I inadvertently precipitated a troublesome reaction. Do you agree?'

'I'm sure you know your responsibilities best.'

McGill allowed the embryonic smile to develop a trifle further, the corners of his eyes crinkling a little.

'That is the attitude I like to see. So as soon as Doctor Hammond returns with his affidavit I will set things in motion.'

Hood nodded and stood up, paused as McGill went on: 'Whatever warnings I may give to the other settlers — and the ranchers in particular — will also apply to you and your fellow developers. I want that clearly understood, Mr

Hood. I do not play favourites. Good day to you, sir.'

* * *

And it *had* been a 'good' day, up until that time, anyway, Hood told himself. He was mighty pleased at the cooperation he had received and the knowledge that he now had somewhere to go for legal redress if or when Cooper tried the rough stuff, which he figured was inevitable.

Not that he was going to run back to McGill with his tail between his legs, whining for help. No, sir!

But he would call on the legal side of things whenever needed. That way he should be able to stay on the right side of this mess, and get on with completing the prove-up.

He had to make sure that Stevens understood, too. Do it legal, get the back-up, and Cooper could do his worst, without making much headway.

If he was really going to become a permanent citizen here, he had to have that kind of assurance.

He was thinking on this, riding back to Anchor, when the first bullet hit.

There was a brief, meaty sound and the buckskin jerked its head violently, grunted and began to go down. The front legs folded first and Hood instantly kicked his boots free of the stirrups and rolled back over the rising rump, instinctively and successfully, from lots of practice, snatching the rifle. It came into his hand almost of its own accord as the horse's falling body moved away from him.

He hit hard, the breath gusting out of him harshly, hat flying, left shoulder striking the ground first. He felt the jerk in his neck and, as he skidded into and partly under a trailside bush, two more shots cracked, gravel and dust spurting. He swung his legs in under the bush, hooked a boot heel on a branch and kicked. The motion threw his body clear, brushing the bush, as lead raked the branches and set twigs and leaves flying.

By then he had wrenched around on his belly, and levered a shell into the breech.

A raking glance up and to his left pinpointed the moving cloud of gun-smoke as his butt nestled firmly against his shoulder. Two cracking shots, one a trifle high, the other lower, ripped into the brush-screened rock, and instantly screamed off in ricochet. It was a fast and accurate action and must have scared the bushwhacker white, not only with the speed of his retaliation, but the closenesss of the bullet.

Even above the dying buckskin's dwindling cries and the rattle of falling gravel, Hood heard the gunman gasp. Then he saw the rifle up there as it sought him again, and his next two shots sent the Winchester's barrel jerking and a man's body erupted from the bush.

He had time to recognize Wilson as the man tumbled and slid and came to a halt, hung up on a deadfall not two yards away. The man's face was towards Hood, blood-streaked, wide-eyed, the mouth working. He had lost his rifle somewhere in the fall.

'Just had to push your luck, didn't you, you dumb bastard,' Hood said, contemptuous of the man's stupidity. Instead of limping away from their previous encounter, hurt but alive, Wilson had got himself killed.

Hood started when the man's eyes, which had been closed, opened abuptly. Wilson started to lift a gravel-grazed hand but the effort was too much for him.

But Hood was just able to make out what he managed to say in gasping, guttural tones.

'No use — me goin' back — an' you still — walkin' around.' He paused, chest heaving as he worked up enough energy to add, 'Fr-Frank woulda — killed me — anyway.'

'Jesus! What a miserable son of a bitch he is.'

Wilson might've heard him but Hood doubted it.

'Not such a hardcase after all. Damn! Now I guess I have to lug you back to town and tell Gus Downie the story, which he might or might not choose to believe.'

Standing over the dead man, Hood hoped Wilson's horse was fit enough to carry them both the few miles back to town.

★   ★   ★

Downie surprised Hood by listening quietly to his story and remaining silent for a short time after he'd finished.

'That it?'

'That's it.'

'Claimin' self-defence, of course.'

'What else? He bushwhacked me.'

'How about the first time?'

'Already told you, Wilson was laying for me. Obviously on Cooper's orders.'

'Not obvious at all. You'd tangled with him before. Your goddam hoss stomped him.'

Hood was tense, even though he had expected a reaction something like this.

'That was when he jumped me. Fact

remains, both times he fired first shot.'

'Yeah, and there's no way to prove that or otherwise, is there?'

'Downie, I don't care whether you believe me or not, but I've told you the truth. I didn't have to bring the body in. Just thought it was the thing to do.'

The hard-faced sheriff had his elbows on his desk chair, fingertips pressed together. He brought his hands back under his stubbled jaw and his eyes were mighty mean.

'You got a strong notion about this 'right thing', ain't you? Don't bother answerin'. I've done some checkin'. You're one tough *hombre*, ain't you? Or figure you are.'

'Listen, what . . . ?'

The lawman flicked a thick finger in a 'stop' sign and Hood met and held Downie's mean stare unflinchingly.

'Used to run guns south of the border with a feller named Concho Bates, didn't you? Sometimes for the Mex Gov'ment, other times for the rebels.'

'Whoever paid most,' Hood told him

quietly, surprised that Downie had dug so deep. 'It was a long time ago.'

The sheriff kept his hard stare on Hood as he sat forward, hands grasping the arms of the chair now.

'You and a Mex *bandido* chief had a fallin' out, I heard. Called himself *El Supremo*. Man who does that has to be plumb loco or mighty confident.' He paused, waited as if for Hood to speak, but when there was no reaction, he continued: 'Your *amigo*, Concho, was a pretty smart *honcho*. When the feud got *real* interesting, he went to this *Supremo* greaser and said you were faster than he was, and if he wanted to prove different, Concho could set up a gunfight between you in an old bullfight arena, charge entry, and — winner take all.'

'Well, the loser wouldn't've been in any condition to make a claim, would he?'

Gus Downie almost smiled. 'Guess not. Made a heap outta that one, din' you?'

'None left, if you're looking for a share.'

Downie scowled now, shaking his head slowly. 'You're one mean streak of piss, all right! No, I'm not lookin' for *dinero*.' He stood abruptly and his right hand lifted swiftly so that Hood slapped his own right hand to his gun butt.

'Hey! Hold up, man. Don't be stupid.'

Hood frowned, reluctant to remove his hand from his gun butt. But he did so when Downie thrust his own hand forward, unmistakably, to grip with Hood, who responded, still a mite leery, but it was a firm, no-nonsense clasp.

He looked into Downie's face, close up now. The lawman said: 'That *El Supremo* bastard wiped out a border mission near Juárez. Killed everyone, includin' the kids. Guns, knives, torture, rape . . . ' He paused and Hood nodded.

'I heard about that.'

Downie held his silence for a long-drawn-out moment, then added with just a trace of a quaver in that harsh, normally gravelly voice: 'My sister was the Mother Superior there. I din' know who you were but I hated your guts for bein' the one to kill *El Supremo*. The scum died too quickly.' He drew down a deep breath. 'Took me a long time to realize how loco I was behavin'. I shoulda been lookin' to buy you a drink, not wantin' to put a bullet in you. That crazy Mex was dead, right? *That*'s what mattered.' Another pause, then: 'Mebbe not too late to buy you that drink?'

Hood stared silently. 'All right with me. And Wilson . . . ?'

'Well, poor old Alby could be a mean sonuver, but never had no brains to speak of. He was like one of them dolls at the travellin' shows: wind 'em up an' let 'em run. He'd do what Cooper told him. This time he ran up agin you.'

It seemed to Hood that, even though Downie's story was true, the man still bore some measure of resentment.

'Tell you what, Downie, I *need* that

drink. I gotta be sure I'm not dreaming this.'

'I'll get the office bottle.' Downie paused as he opened a cupboard door. 'You ain't gonna be sick again all over my floors, I hope?' He asked the question deadpan.

'Depends how much of a drink you gimme.'

The sheriff brought out a bottle and held it up to the light. 'Two-thirds full.'

'Seems about right.' As Downie closed the cupboard Hood asked: 'What're you gonna drink?'

Downie gave him a startled look, and then a slow, crooked smile touched his lips. He shook his head slowly.

'You got more gall than a grizzly.'

After a couple of snorts Hood thought Downie might unwind a little more.

Just the opposite. He corked the bottle, put it away in the cupboard and glared at Hood as he sat down again.

'Mebbe that don't square away your nailin' that *Supremo* scum, but it's all you get from me. Now, I'm willin' to believe your story about Wilson.'

'I'm real pleased to hear that,' Hood said wryly, and Downie's eyes narrowed.

'Listen, I live here. In town I might have certain arrangements with certain people'

'Like Cooper.'

'Like Frank. Them arrangements are between him and me. You get your boots tangled in 'em and you got trouble. For now, Wilson goes on the books as 'Drunk an' homicidal: Now deceased'. That's it. Nothin' else.'

'Leaves it nicely open if you want to add a few gory details, huh?'

Hood waited a few moments before he realized that that *was* it: the sheriff was terminating the meeting. He stood up slowly.

'Well, I guess I'll be goin'.'

'An' keep outta trouble. My conscience is clear now, about you and *Supremo*. Like you said, it was a long time ago, but you got no more credit here. Savvy?'

'Not really,' Hood said honestly, and left.

11

Walls

'Looks to me like you've run up against a brick wall, Frank, ol' pard.' Gus Downie's voice seemed rougher than usual, Cooper thought, as he scowled at the sheriff.

'What the hell're you talkin' about?' Frank Cooper had just lit a cigarillo as he sat on the shaded ranch porch, and he held the vesta a fraction too long. It singed his fingers and he shook the hand violently, accompanied by some inventive curses. 'What wall? Only wall I'm interested in is behind Hood's spread. High, rocky — and damn well outta my reach.'

'Well, it could be that one, but what I meant was, Frank, you've come to a full stop.'

The sheriff was sitting his horse,

leaning on the saddle horn. Wilson's body was draped on a borrowed workhorse behind him and Cooper's attention moved to it. The old bedroll blanket covering him had slipped and showed the man's grey, dirt-smeared face, eyes closed.

'That Alby?' he asked, moving for a better view, and he nodded to himself several times. 'I ain't surprised. Guess he was slow off the mark — again.'

'Mebbe, but the county ain't gonna bury him, Frank. What you do with him is up to you.' Downie gave Cooper a hard look that might have carried some hidden meaning. The rancher stared back, then whistled loudly through his teeth. A sweating man with tongs and a forge-blackened horseshoe appeared in the doorway of the big barn across the ranch yard. Cooper merely jerked a thumb towards the dead man and Downie relinquished the reins when the man set his horseshoe on a bench beside the barn, ran up, and led the horse away.

'You're the goddam sheriff. I hope

you've got Hood in the lock-up while you investigate Wilson's killin'?'

Cooper was mighty edgy.

Downie shook his head. 'Nope. Nothin' to say it was anythin' but a clean shoot-out. 'Course, I ain't examined Alby properly but, like you said, he musta been just too slow. Tell you what, though, that old daisy, McGill, reckons there's been too much trouble already. So he's sendin' for a US Marshal.'

At last the lawman had the big rancher's full attention. Cooper stared a long moment, then made a scoffing sound. 'Wastin' his time.'

'No. He's the land agent, and this is still Federal land, until it's all proved-up and settled. They'll send McGill his marshal all right.'

It was the first time in years that Downie had seen Cooper shaken. He seemed to be breathing harder as he crushed out his cigarillo against the clapboard wall.

'Can't you head him off?'

The sheriff shook his head. 'I'm only a locally elected badge-toter, Frank. My word wouldn't count agin McGill's. 'Sides, I got myself to look out for.'

'Yeah, an' you'll do *that*, won't you? But Judas priest! A goddam federal marshal! — That's the last thing I want to see out here right now!'

'Yeah. Those rannies don't give an inch. An' they can't be bought.'

Cooper's mouth was slightly open, the thick lips twisted. 'He could meet with an accident along the way . . . '

'You loco! Man, you'd have every US Marshal in the country stomping down here.'

'There's gotta be somethin' we can do.'

Downie replied slowly, as if he'd given some long thought to what he was about to say. 'I dunno about this 'we', Frank. I got no hankerin' at all to tangle with the likes of a US Marshal.'

Cooper looked murderous. His nostrils were white-edged as they flared. 'You got an interest in our deal, Gus, damn you! Don't you back out on me now.'

'How can I back out when 'the deal' ain't even properly started? You get things rollin' a damn' sight better'n what they are right now and I'm with you. As things are — uh-uh.' Gus Downie lifted his reins and began to turn his mount. 'I've warned you, Frank. A marshal's comin', hell or high water. You better think about some way of headin' him off that ain't gonna blow up in our — I mean *your* — face. *Adios*.'

As the lawman started to ride away, Cooper came to the rail and gripped it hard, his upper body leaning partway across. 'You're in too deep to get out now, Gus.'

'You know, I thought about that.' Downie slowed his mount, half-hipped in the saddle.

'And?' Cooper cracked.

'Aw, guess I'll give it a leetle more thought.'

'Mebbe you could give some thought to just how Wilson *was* killed . . . ?'

The sheriff reined down, hipped

around further, to look back at the rancher with a hard stare.

'Told you, I ain't had time to examine Alby proper. Din' think it was necessary. He's dead, and we know Hood done it. He ain't even denyin' it.'

'There must be some sign to show *how* he died.' Cooper lowered his voice. 'You know what I mean.'

After a long minute, Downie nodded curtly. 'Believe I do, Frank. But I've toted Wilson back to you. He was your man. *Your* man. I got a chore that'll take me into the Dee-Bar Hills for a spell. You take care of poor old Alby, now, hear? *Adios* again.'

Cooper's face was a gathering thunderstorm as the lawman went on his way. He glared, fists knotted, lips thinned out. Then he became aware of a monotonous *thunking* sound followed by a scraping. Irritably, he looked around and saw Kelly, the man he had called out of the barn earlier, digging a grave on the ridge that shielded the front approach to the ranch house.

Good! Somethin' to gripe about.

'Kelly! Quit that racket!'

He started up the slope as the sweating Kelly — a man with a flabby gut that had cost a good deal in cash and redeye — gladly stopped swinging his pick and leaned on the handle as Cooper came towards him.

Wilson's body lay face down on the old blanket, a film of dust from the digging settling on his clothes.

'Figured this place'd be OK, boss,' Kelly wheezed as the rancher came up.

Cooper said nothing, jammed his cigarillo in a corner of his mouth, and stood over Alby Wilson's body. A few flies were already gathering, but they disappeared entirely when Frank Cooper suddenly drew his six-gun and put two bullets into Wilson's back. Dust spurted from the blanket.

Kelly dropped the pick and jumped back, eyes wide as he stared at the rancher.

'What the hell'd you do that for, boss?'

Cooper's face was deadpan as he reloaded his six-gun and looked coldly at the ranch hand.

'*I* didn't do it,' he said with a twist to his mouth, eyes boring hard into the puzzled Kelly. 'Hood was the one shot poor old Wilson.'

'But — ' Kelly made a kind of helpless gesture. 'He was killed by a rifle bullet, in the chest.'

Cooper nodded, bleak eyes boring into Kelly. 'Yeah, looks like Alby was runnin' away to save his neck, and Hood put two in his back. Musta twisted him as he ran. Gave Hood a chance to shoot him in the chest.'

Kelly licked his lips and swallowed. 'But — was a *rifle* bullet killed him, I said.'

'Well, I guess Hood's Colt was empty after he shot Alby in the back. Must've picked up his Winchester and finished the job when he got spun around. Coulda happened that way.'

'Judas, Frank! I — dunno.'

'*What* don't you know?'

Kelly licked his lips again and saw two or three other ranch hands hurrying over to see what the shooting was about. He wished they'd hurry and get here! Take Frank's attention away from him . . .

'Well, boss, it — it was Gus Downie brung Alby out here an' he didn't have no bullets in his back then.'

'Forget Downie. He'll say what I tell him to — and everyone else better do the same.' Cooper's voice hardened as the first of the other hands came puffing up. Kelly swallowed and hastily nodded.

'Y — You're the boss, Frank.'

Suddenly Cooper smiled: 'You got more brains than I figured, Kel. Just keep usin' 'em and there could be a bonus in your pay this month. Mebbe for all you fellers.'

Kelly knew that was meant to make them feel better about this: after all, Wilson *had* been one of them originally.

But, although Kelly answered Frank's smile, stiffly, he still felt kind of queasy as he looked at those gaping holes in Alby Wilson's back.

Someone better be able to explain them away, especially with a US Marshal to satisfy.

★ ★ ★

Hood thought Trish's hand trembled — just slightly — when she poured his second cup of coffee.

He was seated at the plank table in the cabin and Stevens had just come in, mopping his face with a piece of cloth after obviously having doused his head before entering.

'Man! It ain't full summer yet and I reckon I've lost ten pounds in two days tryin' to clear them boulders so we can get to the north edge easier.'

'I've made some lemonade,' Trish said. 'You'd prefer that to coffee, Steven?'

'I'll say.' He sat down while she went to a jug in the kitchen area, asking Hood if he wanted any lemonade, but he shook his head.

Hood rolled a cigarette and pushed the makings towards Stevens, who made a smoke of his own. He drank the lemonade before sharing Hood's match, looking at him through the smoke.

'You been gone a while.'

'Picked up a little news here and there.' Hood told them about his visit to Doc Hammond and the replica Spanish maps he had on his wall. 'It looks promising. Can't really make out anything for sure but for a couple of Spanish words that mean 'wall' or 'walls'. But whatever, it was all on this land, if that badlands trail ever existed.'

'Does that mean we'll be able to find this — what is it? A legend? Just a rumour or — what?' Trish asked.

Hood looked sharply at her. 'Your guess is as good as mine. Doc seems to know about it but I'm not sure whether he actually believes there was such a trail.'

'But if there is?' she insisted.

Hood shrugged. 'If there is, and we

can find it — and clear it, we could make ourselves a little spending money by using it to get our cattle to Socorro before anyone else.'

Stevens whistled softly. The girl stared uncertainly, wondering if such good fortune was too much to hope for, considering the hand life had dealt her so far.

Suddenly, Hood realized he had been saying 'our' quite naturally while he was talking about what could be done. It gave him a bit of a start but he decided that that was OK. He'd never intended to have partners, but things seemed to be working out that way, hopefully for the better. *Our team, our land.* Sounded pretty good.

'Will there be any trouble over this man Wilson who tried to ambush you?' Trish asked.

Hood shook his head. 'I doubt it. Downie seemed to accept my story after initially being suspicious. If there's any fuss maybe it'll land in Cooper's lap. But he'll deny that he sent Wilson to bushwhack me, anyway.'

'Seems the arrival of this US Marshal might settle things down some,' opined Stevens, draining his coffee, then finishing the mouthful of cold lemonade he had left. 'I could use a hand with a couple of big boulders, Hood. You got time?'

'Time — and a couple sticks of dynamite I've been saving. Just don't ask where I got 'em, 'cause they didn't cost me anything.'

Stevens smiled but Trish looked a trifle surprised at the implied admission of theft: petty, maybe, but . . .

* ★ ★

The explosion was noisy, brief, and sent up a veritable fountain of debris, mostly dirt and small brush. It split the huge, stubborn boulder into pieces of a size the two men could manage to move.

'How about we keep the second stick for this badlands trail, if we can find it?' suggested Stevens.

Hood wiped sweat from his forehead and looked sharply at the other man. 'Don't get too hopeful about it, Steve. It might not even be there. Doc's interpretation of the marks on his so-called map don't look like much more than smears to me; could mean anything.'

'Thought you'd be more optimistic than that.'

'I've had my moments, but mostly what I own or have had has come because I've worked for it. But let's take a quick look and see if we can find anything to really raise our hopes.'

'Now you're talkin'!'

★   ★   ★

They sat their mounts on a low ridge, looking out towards the sloping, crumbling part of the massive natural wall.

'By God! Now *that* is what I call a landslide!' exclaimed Stevens.

Hood nodded. 'Doc says there was always a rumour that the Spaniards blew

167

down the top of the wall while a big band of Comanches were comin' through the pass that was originally here. Whatever, she's sure choked off any pass now.'

Stevens didn't seem to be listening. He spurred his mount to the edge of the massive pile of rocks, then dismounted and began to climb up.

'Hey, watch it, Steve,' Hood called warningly. 'They might not be secure.'

Stevens merely waved without looking back, and climbed higher and higher. Hood, becoming agitated, worried that there might be another landslide, with Steve riding it.

Then Stevens turned and came back, jumping from one high rock to a lower one, actually setting one rolling. Hood felt his throat close, waiting for the underpinning rocks to collapse, but in minutes Steve was standing beside his mount, sweating, clothes soiled from the climb, a small piece of broken rock in his hand.

He dusted off, slapping at his clothes with his hat. 'Wasn't bein' stupid.

Thought that rock looked kinda igneous and I wanted a look at where it had originally broken away from.' He pointed vaguely up the slope of piled rocks and boulders to a dark, shadow-like crescent.

'What sort of rock did you say it was?' Hood asked, taking the small sample from Stevens and examining it.

'Igneous. Aw, it only means it was originally formed by a lot of heat: a volcano, probably. See, it's sort of granular. That dark lip way up at the top of the pile likely was a lava tunnel, way, way back, I reckon, exposed when this landslide happened, whether the Spaniards did it, or God.'

'Yeah?' Hood sounded kind of vague, not sure what Stevens was getting at.

'What I'm sayin' is, that there was likely one huge tunnel, maybe runnin' clear through the wall or deep into it, and whatever happened, it got filled or blocked off with this mess of rocks.' He waved a hand around at the huge pile.

'So, the Spaniards filled up the trail

to get away from the Indians? Is that it?'

'Could be, but 'why' don't matter. Just that whatever was here has been blocked off for ever with the amount of rock that came down. The wall itself could've been part of a volcanic cone, I guess, thousands of years ago, I mean.'

Hood frowned. 'How come you know so much about rock?

Stevens looked surprised. 'Hell, didn't mean to lecture! I worked for a spell with a big minin' company in Wyoming and we did a heap of tunnel work. Some of the machinery they had would clear most of this in a week. They brought it in from England, bits at a time, and assembled it where they wanted to work. Had lots of know-how, those gophers, as they called themselves.'

'So you don't think there really was a 'Badlands Trail'? Just a tunnel which might or might not have been large enough to drive cattle through?'

'Oh, could've been. I mean, that might just be the roof of a big cavern up there, but if it was a tunnel . . . well, it might've gone right through and come out above the badlands — or grassy plains as they likely were that far back.' He suddenly looked concerned. 'Aw, Judas, Hood! You look disappointed. Damn! Didn't mean to . . . '

Hood lifted a hand, smiled thinly. 'It's OK, Steve. This is more the story of my life than the other way round. Thanks for tellin' me what you know. I hadn't a notion.'

'Well, I din' know it when we were plannin' on makin' a short cut to Socorro.'

Hood's smile softened some. 'Cooper apparently doesn't, either.'

After a few seconds' pause Stevens grinned.

'No, he don't, do he? I hope he likes surprises!'

They both laughed.

12

The Marshal

Lucas McGill looked up sharply from the land deed he was adding to his register in his neat writing, and saw a man about his own age, height and build standing holding the office door, which he had opened with a crash.

McGill could smell the trail dust on his crumpled clothes from across the room.

'You the agent?' the newcomer asked in a rough, deep voice that some small men often had.

'I am *Mister* Lucas McGill, land agent for this county. Yes. And who, sir, might you be?'

The man reached into a vest pocket and tossed something that landed lumpily on McGill's pile of papers beside his forearm, making him jump a little.

'Evan Ward,' the newcomer said, nodding to whatever he had tossed on to the desk and which was now lost among sliding papers. 'That's 'who'; the other tells you what.'

McGill frowned, obviously annoyed, and he searched for the 'other' object that this Evan Ward had thrown so peremptorily. He started at a sharp jab in his hand and bit back a short curse as he picked up a heavy silver badge with the words *US Marshal* engraved across the front.

He thrust himself to his feet, surprise showing on his face. 'What — what're you doing here? I only sent a wire yesterday.'

'Caught me between jobs. Had just left Socorro and was heading home when a wire from headquarters caught up with me and ordered me to Hadleyville.' Ward sported a heavy moustache and it gave a sort of twitch as he added, 'You got some pull, I guess?'

'Pull? If you mean 'influence', well, I

rather like to think it's more 'reputation' that has bred its due respect.'

'My God!' Ward said, dropping into the visitor's chair and using his hat to slap a little dust from the trousered leg he hooked across one knee. 'You talk like that Webster — the feller who wrote the lexicon.'

'You flatter me,' McGill said wryly and half-rose, leaning across the desk and thrusting out his right hand. His face softened. 'I'm very pleased you're here, Marshal. Welcome to Hadleyville.'

Ward grunted, giving McGill's hand a perfunctory shake, thumbing back his hat now. 'You got some trouble, huh?'

'Some — yes. But I foresee a . . . well, 'range war' may be too strong a term, but — '

'You figure it's possible,' cut in the lawman. 'OK. Range wars and lynchin's are my speciality, so put me in the picture.'

McGill smiled openly now. 'A pleasure. You don't know what a relief it is that you've arrived so soon.'

'Yeah. A long, dry ride it was, too, to get here.'

It only took a split second for McGill to identify the hint for a drink — *not water!* He rose and went to a polished wall cupboard, paused with the door halfway open.

'Which would you prefer? Rye, bourbon, brandy? All bonded stock, I assure you.'

Ward heaved himself to his feet and crossed the room to stand beside McGill, his eyes lighting up at the sight of the rows of bottles in the cupboard.

He grinned.

'Hey, now! Let's you and me sit down and discuss this . . . problem you have — in detail, I mean. Gimme the whole story from the beginnin'. Oh, an' I reckon I'll start with a snort of . . . did you say bonded bourbon? Aaaaah, yes! Let's start with that, huh?'

McGill's smile by this time was kind of sickly.

★　★　★

'The marshal's here already?'

Hood blinked as Steve told him the news.

'Yeah. Feller who brung that small stove you ordered for Trish — and for which I thank you, Hood — said he come in last night. Named Evan Ward. You know him?'

'Heard of him.'

'Good man. Nothin' to look at, but gets the job done. Likes to pull a cork or two. They say he once drank a full bottle of whiskey, then walked straight as a die into the street and, with them Smith & Wessons of his, blasted all five of Drag O'Hara's gang. Then went back inside yellin' for more whiskey — said he was thirsty after all that work.'

Hood smiled. 'Yeah, I've heard a few stories. Hope he's been properly briefed on the trouble here.'

'He's with McGill.'

Hood nodded. 'He'll need a drink after having his ear bent by him. But he'll get the full story, I reckon. McGill's a bit of an old woman, but he takes his job seriously.'

He paused, frowning at the enquiring look on Stevens's face. 'What is it?'

'Just wonderin' if I should kinda slip into town and lay in a stock of bourbon, 'case Ward decides to visit.'

Hood grinned. 'Hope you can pay for it. I'm about bust, an' I still owe for the stove.'

Stevens's face straightened. 'Oh, damn! I'm flat broke, too.'

'If he comes, feed him some of Trish's apple pie.'

★　★　★

Frank Cooper slammed a fist down on to the scarred eating table in his bunkhouse and growled a curse.

'G-a-w-d dammit! How the hell'd they get a marshal here so blamed quick? No, no, never mind. Don't matter *how*, the sonuver's here, that's what matters.' He glared at Blackie Tallant, who had brought him the news from town. 'You see him?'

'Yeah, Frank. It's Ward, all right. Seen him in Abilene once. Christ! He's sizzlin'-fast with them guns. Not only that, he hits what he aims for.'

'McGill got him under his wing, I guess?'

Tallant smiled crookedly. 'Booked him into Fluffy Flo's, the Heaven-or-Hell suite. They say McGill's face was red as a midsummer sundown when he paid over the money.'

That news didn't even raise a smile from Cooper.

He rubbed a hand around his bristly jowls. 'Well, I reckon we can safely say he won't be leavin' town tonight. But I think I'll be on hand early when our marshal surfaces in the mornin'!'

'Be more like high noon, if Flo's handlin' things herself tonight.'

Cooper didn't seem to hear, deep in thoughts of his own. 'The ice house take care of Wilson's body all right?'

'Reckon so, but Judd Cress is gonna charge you — says you shoulda brung it in earlier. Startin' to smell some an' his customers don't care for a corpse bein' . . . '

'I'll worry about Cress later. I gotta try and figure somethin' with this damn marshal. I ain't planning on locking horns with him if I can help it.'

'You got them two extra holes in Alby's back to work a story around.' Blackie spoke stiffly; Wilson had been a bunkhouse pard of his and he didn't take kindly to the way his corpse was being treated.

Now he felt his stomach tighten as Cooper bored a bleak stare into him.

'You come with me into town tomorrow.'

'Judas, Frank! I been runnin' around like the goddam Pony Express!'

'And if that's what I want you to do you'll do it. Right?'

Tallant tightened his thin lips, badly wanting to make some sort of retort, but he could see he was already treading on thin ice, so he merely sighed and nodded.

* * *

It was Flo herself who opened the door to Frank Cooper's knock: big, buxom, middle-aged, with faded face paint and dark crescents showing beneath her eyes.

A huge mass of black hair piled up on her head added inches to her actual height; she seemed mighty weary to him.

'Oh, Frank! Well, well, well, long time no see. When're you coming to visit me again?'

'When I recover from the last time,' Cooper said, unable to maintain his sour mood: not with this woman, who could take any man on that proverbial journey where he felt he had died and gone to Heaven, and then come back for more.

She threw a quick glance over her shoulder, then forced a smile. 'You're kind of early, Frank . . . ' she prompted him.

'Lookin' for the US Marshal. He awake yet?'

'*Awake?* I served him a breakfast I would normally call my most expensive supper and had to send one of my gals down to the hotel to charm the cook out of a second beefsteak, and . . . well, never mind. Yes. He's awake, maybe just having a light snooze.' She lowered her voice. 'Whatever business you have with him, Frank, take him with you, will you?'

'Don't tell me you've found a man who's too much for you, Flo.'

'Hell, no! It's not that. He says to bill the county. They sent for him and he always works 'expenses paid'. You know how much damn chance I've got of collectin' for what he wants to spend!'

Cooper laughed. 'I better see him, Flo.' He turned to Blackie Tallant. 'You go tell Judd Cress to get Wilson outta the icebox or wherever he put him.'

*   *   *

Marshal Ward looked spry enough as he sat over coffee, smoking a cheroot, reading some sort of letter or paper. He nodded to Cooper.

'Mornin', Marshal. Sorry to interrupt your meal or whatever, but I got me a little problem.'

'Don't look so little to me.' Ward tapped the paper and Frank's mouth tightened some as he recognized McGill's neat writing: the agent's report! 'You got a dead man on your hands, too, they tell me.'

'Yeah! One of my best hands, Alby Wilson. Him and some Johnny-come-lately callin' himself 'Hood' have been at loggerheads over somethin'. I dunno the full story. But seems they shot it out along the trail and Hood killed Alby. Well, I guess, these things happen, but when they brung Alby in with a couple bullets in his back . . . ' The marshal snapped his head up at that. 'I got my dander up. Lucky you showed up — you can investigate, but if you hadn't been on your way, I reckon me and Hood mighta gone head to head.'

The lawman smiled crookedly, gave

his head just one small shake. 'Someone was lucky, right enough.'

Cooper flushed, but retained control.

Ward tapped his paper. 'This is McGill's report, but I've seen Sheriff Downie's, too. Neither mentions bullets in the back. They say Wilson was killed by a shot in the chest: front of the chest. And this Hood feller don't deny puttin' it there.'

'Hell, Marshal! That could be, and that mighta finished him. I reckon them two bullets in his back would've spun him and then Hood nailed him in the chest.'

'Changed his Colt for a rifle, eh?' Ward pursed his lips, stifled a half-yawn. He smiled. 'Late night. Frank, I got Sheriff Downie's report and he don't mention Wilson was shot in the back.'

'Well, when he brung Alby out to my ranch he was wrapped in an old blanket. Gus might not've seen the bullet holes.' Cooper knew he was on safe ground here: he had changed the blanket for an old bedroll blanket that had no bullet holes in it. 'Gus said he never examined Alby because, accordin' to Hood, it was a square shoot-out and Hood wasn't tryin' to dodge the issue.'

Cooper kind of smiled and shrugged, spreading his hands. 'Can only tell you what I know, Marshal. But Gus Downie can likely explain it better.'

Marshal Ward looked at Cooper steadily, without speaking, for a long, uncomfortable minute. 'He could. But I hear he's somewhere in the Dee-Bar Hills, on some sort of chore?'

Cooper chuckled, making Ward arch his eyebrows quizzically. 'Yeah! A chore like takin' care of the needs of a certain half-Commanche squaw who works on the reservation. But you never heard that from me.'

'Uh-huh. Tell you what, you got a couple sawbones in this town as can do more'n just take a splinter out of a man's thumb?'

Frowning, Frank Cooper nodded slowly. 'Yeah, sure.'

'How many?' When Frank held up three fingers, the lawman nodded. 'Bring 'em in here and I'll have 'em look at the body.'

'What good'll that do?' Frank asked quickly.

'Just bring 'em. An' tell someone I'd like a strong cup of coffee with a snort of brandy on the side.'

Doc Hammond was the man to listen to: Ward figured that as soon as he saw how the other two medics, one old, one young, deferred so readily to Hammond and showed him real respect.

'Marshal, we're all agreed,' Hammond told the lawman after examining Alby Wilson. 'The rifle bullet in the chest caused Wilson's death. The two pistol shots in the back could well have proved fatal, except they happened after Wilson was dead.'

Marshal Evan Ward grew a couple of inches as he straightened at this news. He raked his stare over the trio of medics and the other two nodded in agreement with Doc Hammond.

'You're sure, then?'

'Absolutely. There's been no bleeding into the tissue, Marshal,' said the young medic, called Benson. He poked at the nearest wound with a bright metal instrument that resembled a screwdriver, except it had a small hook on the end. 'See? Desiccated.'

'The hell's that?'

'Er, kind of dried out, crumbly almost. The blood had drained from that tissue long before those two bullets were administered.' Doc Hammond glanced at Cooper, who looked a mite pale, tight-faced.

'Hey! Hey, wait up! I — I don't like the sounds of this.' He made himself look and sound bewildered. 'Gus brought the body to me wrapped in a blanket — this is the way it was. He did say he hadn't examined Alby closely because it was obvious the rifle bullet had killed him. But . . . ' He shrugged again. 'I dunno what else to tell you, Marshal.'

Ward kept his gaze on Cooper's face

but the big rancher didn't flinch: he knew Downie would make sure he couldn't be contacted for a few days. Cagey man, the sheriff, and one not keen to add more work to his load.

'I can only give you my word, Marshal, and that of a couple of my men who were with me when Downie brought poor Wilson out to us. One's my foreman, Will Oberon. He's a highly respected cattleman and — '

'I know of Oberon. I'll be questioning him along with the rest of your crew, and whoever else can help me in this town.'

'Er, how long will this take, Marshal? I mean, I run a workin' ranch and we're getting ready for roundup.'

'Shouldn't take long, Frank. Fact, I can save time by startin' with you right now. Gimme what you know and I'll have something to compare the others' stories to. You happy with that?'

Far from it! thought Cooper, but what choice did he have?

He forced a smile and worked hard at

making his answer casual: 'Whatever you say, Marshal. I'll get the boys to slaughter a steer and we'll have us a good old Texas-style barbecue and wing-ding tonight.'

Marshal Evan Ward merely nodded, his thoughts elsewhere. *Who in hell would want to shoot a dead man?* he wondered. *Trying to make it look bad for this Hood . . . ?*

'One of my men, Lon Kelly, was about to bury Wilson, when the blanket slipped and he noticed the bullet holes in his back,' Cooper said suddenly. 'I didn't know if Hood had put 'em there but figured I'd better play it safe, which is why I took Wilson to the ice house, so's he'd be fit for you to look at when you got here.'

'That was a good idea, Frank. This Kelly around?'

'Aw, shoot!' Cooper snapped his fingers and shook his head slowly. 'I sent him up into the ranges, chousing mavericks. I'm sick of all these squatters nibbling away at my range an' stockin' their damn spreads with my mavericks. I reckon it — '

'When'll Kelly be back?' cut in the marshal.

'Kel . . . ? Aw, few days, long as it takes for him to clear as many mavericks as he can down to my home pastures an' chase some of them sons of bi — '

'Uh-huh,' Ward cut in again; not interested in Cooper's maverick problems. 'When you can, send a man to bring this Kelly in soon's possible.'

Frank nodded quickly. 'Sure, Marshal, whatever you say.'

'Hold that thought an' we'll get along fine.'

'I could go myself, I s'pose . . . '

'Don't let me keep you.'

13

Death on the Range

Lon Kelly was an easy-going man, in the main: happy being told what to do, thus saving himself the effort of thinking things out for himself; perhaps 'lazy' might be a better description than 'easy-going', after all.

He liked company, especially if decisions had to be made. He might seem as if he was helping to decide things but mostly it was just easy agreement with whoever his companion happened to be.

Frank Cooper was his boss and Kelly had always got along well enough with him by agreeing without argument. He hadn't particularly wanted this maverick-watching chore, but he had given it some thought when Cooper had first ordered him into the ranges.

Hell, he had seen Frank shoot poor

Alby Wilson — already dead, mind! and while he figured Frank must have his reasons, Kelly didn't want to try to figure them out.

When he had been given this chore it had suited him fine: whatever the outcome of the back-shooting was not now his concern. So he could chase down the few mavericks in this area and make certain-sure they were well within Cooper's boundaries. And stayed there.

Easy!

But even though Kelly's brain wasn't used to much exercise there were times when it made him stop and actually think. Like why Cooper had to do that to Alby.

They had been saddlemates on and off for years, Kelly and Wilson, and had been pleased to discover they were both on Cooper's payroll with easy-to-handle jobs that allowed them to spend a good deal of time together for a Saturday night on the town, even an occasional afternoon's fishing.

Their relationship never grew any

closer than that; if one wanted to do something different from the other, well, that was fine, they would go their separate ways for whatever time it took.

He was a paid gun at times whenever Frank ordered it, but that never bothered Lon Kelly: usually it meant a 'bonus' in the monthly pay. He knew Alby Wilson had been doing some chore that Frank thought was important, but he had no details, and damn well didn't want 'em, either!

Whatever it was, had got Alby killed, and even then he wasn't allowed to rest in peace. Man, that galled him! Riding along a low ridge, Kelly suddenly stopped his mount as that particular thought came into his head.

Yeah! Alby had died for Frank, and his reward wasn't even a decent burial. No, it was two extra bullets in his back and being humped around from place to place, even shoved into the iceworks. And Alby was a man who hated the cold.

It came to Lon Kelly then that it was

up to him to do something about that kind of — desecration? Was that the word he wanted? Didn't matter, *he* knew what he meant and had finally allowed the thought to filter through into his mind.

'By hell! It just ain't right!'

He said this out loud, surprised that he had done so much figuring for himself . . .

'What ain't right, Lon?'

Kelly almost toppled from the horse, he spun so fast in the saddle. His eyes widened and his belly knotted when he saw Big Frank Cooper sitting one of his own large mounts, a big-rumped grey, at the edge of some brush fringing the trail, his rifle across his legs, one big hand on the action.

'Judas, Frank! You damn near made me wet my pants.'

Cooper grinned. 'Somethin' to see in a grown man, eh? How's the maverick huntin' goin'?'

'Aw, only got five so far. Put 'em in that little draw down the slope. Can't quite see it from here.'

He half-stood in the stirrups as he pointed and Frank did the same. 'You mean that one near the trail up to the wall? Hell! That's almost on Hood's section. If he's a mind he could take them mavericks and have his brand slapped on 'em before we could spit.'

Kelly looked alarmed at the anger in Cooper's voice.

'But we've used it before and — hey, Frank!'

He yelled this last but the word was cut off by the gunshot as Cooper fired his rifle, barely lifting it from across his thighs.

Lon Kelly was punched clear over the horse's rump and the animal stomped in fright before lunging away — one shoe making a mess of Kelly's already contorted face.

'Goddam! That was a real fancy shot.' Frank leaned a little out of the saddle, looking down at Kelly. 'Just in case you figured whatever you was sayin' '*ain't right*' ought to be passed along to that marshal, Lon, an' you're the only one seen me shoot Alby. Hey! I used my rifle an' we're within easy rifle shot of Hood's place here, just over that other trail. Aw, Hood, you poor son of a bitch! Are you gonna have some explainin' to do to Marshal Evan Ward when he hears *my* story about what happened to poor ol' Kelly here!'

★   ★   ★

Hood reined down just within the line of trees where Stevens was setting the top crossbar in place on the small holding corral. There were three steers, still a mite edgy from being driven into the corral, and not a brand mark anywhere on their dusted, scuffed hides. Not yet.

'These fellers been hidin' in the brush, I reckon,' Stevens called as Hood rode up. 'Still got some stickin' to — '

'You hear that gunshot, minute or two back?'

Stevens sobered. 'Did hear somethin'. Could've been a shot, I guess. I was concentratin' on gettin' them mavericks on our side of the trail.' He quickly scanned the rising ground well behind Hood, the brushline spreading into a treed area, all on Cooper's ranch. 'Someone workin' up there, mebbe?'

'Dunno. But sure I heard a rifle. Was hopin' Coop or one of his men weren't takin' potshots at you. We're close as we come to his line here.'

'Nope, ain't seen anyone. An' these here mavericks musta leaned on them bob-wire posts until the wire slacked off enough for 'em to step across. Guess our grass looks sweeter.'

'This part of the range it is. Look at 'em. They'll have it wore down to stubble by sundown, way they're going at it.'

Stevens had been studying Cooper's slope and nodded a trifle absently. 'Don't see anyone. Coulda just been one of his men takin' a shot at a varmint. Don't look like they're interested in us, anyway.'

'No.' Hood glanced at the sky. As he did they both heard a distant *bonging* and Hood smiled. 'Trish — right on time. My belly's growling like a starvin' grizzly's — and there goes the kitchen triangle. Wonder you ain't heavier than you are, Steve, way she cooks so good.'

'Well, you'll be puttin' on weight, the size of the platefuls she serves you.'

Hood grinned. 'You won't hear me complainin'. Come on. We'll look for more mavericks after we've filled our bellies. Wanna race?'

Their horses both gave startled snorts as the spurs touched home and sent them tearing away across Anchor land towards the distant cabin.

As they rounded the first bend and dropped from sight in the dip of the land, a rider eased his horse out of the treeline on the top of the rise.

It was Frank Cooper and he grinned tightly.

'Enjoy your lunch, you sonuvers. With any luck it'll be the last one you have this side of Hell.'

Doc Hammond frowned a little as he looked at Marshal Evan Ward.

'I don't think even a full autopsy would tell us for sure just when Alby Wilson was shot in the back, Marshal. I wouldn't even try to estimate at what time he was killed, not now he's been kept on ice for so long and has thawed again. But if you do wish for a complete autopsy, I'll need some assistance and . . . '

Ward, beads of sweat now showing on his creased forehead, held up a hand. 'Hold it, Doc!' He paused, thinking about what he was going to say next. Hammond jumped when the lawman slapped both hands to his holstered six-guns.

'Relax, Doc. Just wanna say I never use a shot gun. I got no use for bustin' a man apart and seein' his innards.' He paused, swallowed, clapped his hands on his gun butts again. 'I stick to my old friends, Smith an' Wesson. If I can't stop a man with them, then he's either damn lucky or I'm unlucky. You savvy what I'm saying, Doc?'

Hammond nodded slowly. The feared Marshal Ward was telling him in his own way that he was plain queasy and did not want to see any human being dissected.

'That's between you and me, Doc. You know your medical oath, huh? All's private between you and your patients, right?'

Hammond did his best to keep a straight face as he nodded. 'Of course, Marshal. Don't give it another thought.'

'Oh, I will. An' I hope you will, too.' Those bleak eyes that had watched dozens of men go to their Maker, violently, steadied on Hammond's face and then they warmed — a little.

'You'd be a good man to tell me a few things, I reckon, Doc.'

'If I can. Always remembering my privacy oath, of course.'

The lawman almost smiled. 'Ah! You're on the ball, Doc. But you can tell me what I want to know, like what you think of this Frank Cooper. I know he's got a reputation for ridin' over folk roughshod and thinks the sun shines outta his nether regions, but I've known men like that before and they usually have a couple of good traits, to kinda compensate. But, from what I've picked up around here, Frank Cooper seems to get by just by scarin' folk — or threatening 'em. That accurate?'

'Look, Marshal, what you say about Cooper is . . . well, with a mild reservation here and there, I guess it sums him up. But there's always a lot of talk about a man like that in any community when he's a success and is resented for it. Some of the things that're said are pretty wild and, as far as I know, have never actually been proved.'

Ward's moustache twitched and Hammond guessed the man had really given a small smile this time.

'You sound like every damn sawbones I've ever met. Like drawin' teeth to get him to tell you time of day.

Always leaves room for doubt.'

'Isn't that the law, Marshal? A man is innocent until proven guilty?'

Ward's eyes narrowed again and the moustache drooped normally now. 'An' you know how many sons of bitches have got off their crimes because of *that*.' He touched the butt of his right hand Smith & Wesson. 'If I have any doubt, I consult my old pard — and his pard — right here!'

Hammond remained silent, wanting to get away from this lawman who seeemed to be a little more complex than he had first appeared. Then, suddenly, Evan Ward started speaking in an almost confidential tone: 'Find it kind of irritating, that Sheriff Downie has gone and lost himself in some damn hills just before I arrived. Then this feller Kelly, who was going to bury Wilson and must've noticed those bullets in his back, is sent out to some damn backwoods to round up mavericks. Downie I know as a so-so lawman, eager to protect his back at all times.

OK. This Lon Kelly, if he's the one I'm thinkin' of, also looks after Number One, usually with his hand stretched out just far enough to hold a fistful of cash . . . Them things, added to Frank Cooper's reputation — well, to me, it raises a kind of stink. You with me, Doc?'

'Er, your reasoning seems . . . reasonable, Marshal. But I don't see how I can help you.'

'You can. Gimme your picture of this Hood. You must know him pretty well if you can bring back his memory.'

'Oh, now wait up! His memory returned of its own accord. It was a natural occurrence.'

'Because of the treatment you gave him. Don't hide your light under a bushel, Doc Hammond. You got a reputation well beyond this county, and it's a good one. I can read Cooper a little and I get the notion he'd be more'n happy if he could put blame of some sort on this Hood. Now, you know Hood better'n anyone else, and if you don't want to see him tossed in the cooler — and that's where he's headed if I listen to Big Frank — then you'll put me in the true picture.'

Hammond frowned. 'It'll still be just my own opinion and — I'll be honest, Marshal — I'm biased. I like Hood. He's tough and he's a fighter, and, in my opinion, he's a straight-shooter.'

'An' he hangs up his wings every night before turnin' in, I s'pose.'

Hammond glared, then softened his look. 'He's no angel, but he has a rare sense of fair play and — and *honesty* that you don't find all that often out here.'

'And not just out here. All right, Doc. I like to get all sides to a man if I can. And from what I can gather, Hood may be being set up like a clay pigeon.'

'If he is I don't need to ask who by.'

Ward smiled that twitchy smile again and started to speak as the door burst open and a sweating, dusty, panting Frank Cooper stumbled in with a man in cow-puncher's outfit, looking just as frazzled.

'Marshal!' gasped Cooper. His face straightened when he recognized the medic but he flicked his eyes to the lawman and, chest heaving, sputtered: 'He just shot Lon Kelly.'

Hammond frowned but Ward kept a straight face.

'Kelly? He's the feller who noticed the bullets in Wilson's back?' he asked, and Cooper, trying to get his breath, nodded vigorously. He jerked a thumb at the cowpuncher, who was regarding the lawman warily.

'Yeah, yeah, when he was gettin' ready to bury him. But, Marshal, this is one of my top hands, Virg Keene, and he's been helping Lon. Well hell, Virg, don't leave it all to me. You're the one seen it happen.'

It was plain Virg wished he hadn't, or wasn't quite sure what he was supposed to say, but he stumbled through a meandering story which boiled down to this: he and Kelly had been checking the fences that marked Cooper's boundary up the slope from the trail that led to their nearest neighbour: Hood's Anchor. They heard cattle bawling and a couple of men shouting, but kind of subdued, as if they didn't really want to be heard from too far away.

Kelly yelled at Virg to tie off his wire and follow him to investigate. Virg was halfway there, he figured, still in the treeline, when he heard Kelly yell: 'What you fellers, doin' there? Don't cut that fence, Goddammit! Hey! I'm talkin' to you, Hood.'

'An' — an' I heard a rifle shot an' hauled rein so I was still screened in the trees, an' there was Kel lyin' on the ground, twitchin', and Hood was sittin' his bronc with a smokin' rifle in his hands. That feller he has workin' for him, Steve someone, was further down the slope and he yelled, soundin' real mad, too: 'Judas priest, Hood! The hell've you done?'

'I din' hear what Hood said,' Virg concluded, not quite so tongue-tied now. 'I stayed put. Figured he'd put a bullet into me, too, if I showed myself.

'They'd been cuttin' my fences, and there was tracks, and some cows were still millin' about, where they'd been drivin' mavericks off my land on to free range, between our spreads, which made 'em legal to collect.'

Ward studied Virg until the man started to squirm, then he looked at the impatient rancher.

'Looks like I better go see this Hood pronto. You come along, Frank, and you I guess, Virg.'

'Aw, hell! I — I don't want Hood to know I seen what he done,' protested Virg Keene, looking appealingly at his boss.

'Yeah, might be best if Hood din' know there was a witness, eh, Marshal?'

Hard eyes bored into Cooper. 'That how you figure it? Well, I don't, but leave it go — for now. Long as this feller here don't get sent into some wild country or on an errand where he can't be reached if I want to check his story.'

Frank Cooper stiffened, did his best to keep a straight face as the Marshal said, 'Go back to the ranch and wait, Virg. Frank, be quiet! This is my chore, you just do like you're told and we'll go see Hood. Before we leave, send someone to bring in Kelly's body.'

'He's outside,' Frank snapped, obviously not happy at being put down by the marshal. 'Draped over a hoss.'

'Then let's take a look before we leave for Hood's place.'

Ward nodded to the silent doctor: 'You better come, too, Doc. Too bad you ain't the local undertaker: you'd be gettin' rich, livin' around here.'

'I won't get rich or otherwise if I don't go back and see my patients, Marshal. Sorry. You'll have to do what you have to do without me.'

'Goddammit, Doc! I — '

He stopped in mid-complaint as Hammond held up a hand. 'I can help you out a little, Marshal. Hood's not far away, apparently, and he'll know when he delivered the killing shot to Wilson. Frank here must have some idea when Kelly noticed the bullet holes in

Wilson's back. I can probably give you a rough estimate of when that happened, using those times. Best I can do, I'm afraid.'

Ward still looked surly but he jerked a nod. 'All right. Dunno if it'll help but time of death is always important.'

'Judas!' Cooper said tautly. 'Sounds more like a witch doctor at work to me!'

Ward glared. 'And I've had a couple of *them* help me out real good, Frank. You go do what you have to, Doc, and lemme have those times soon as you can. All right with you, Frank?'

Cooper could do nothing but nod.

Nobody had anything to say to that as Ward swung impatiently towards the door. But Doc Hammond's lips tightened: he had hoped he might be left behind so he could make some attempt to warn Hood.

This smelled of some kind of a set-up to him.

14

Run For It!

Hood straightened and rubbed at his aching lower back, then lifted his hat slightly with one hand and wiped his shirtsleeve across his sweating face.

'Reckon that'll do, Steve. We've got room for a few more, but I don't want to give Cooper a chance to bring the marshal in 'cause he's complainin' I'm runnin' too many of his mavericks on Anchor.'

'All right by me,' gasped Stevens, dropping another cross rail in the small corral they had built. 'Long as we have enough to make up a small herd and get it on the trail to Socorro early so we get a decent price.'

'Yeah, well I like operatin' that way. Seen a lot of fellers go under from bein' too greedy, buildin' their herds with someone else's mavericks, because they — Hey! Visitor.'

Hood shaded his eyes to study the rider approaching through the trees. 'It's Doc. Figured he'd be back in Hadleyville by now.' He lifted an arm and waved and Hammond returned the gesture, set his mount upslope to where Hood and Stevens were working.

When he arrived he lost no time in asking Hood if he could recall when he'd shot it out with Wilson.

'I don't normally keep tally of such things but I reckon it was . . . Wednesday. Yeah, last Wednesday.'

'The day's not so important, Hood. The time of day is.'

Hood looked mildly surprised and frowned as he gave the matter some thought. 'Would've been 'bout half-hour before high noon. Recall usin' the shadows to get a line on Alby's movements. Because the sun was so high above he likely figured he wouldn't throw much of a shadow, I guess. But he did. Enough to cause a bulge in the outline of a rock

210

he was hiding behind. That near enough, Doc?'

'It is for me. And I think Marshal Ward'll be satisfied.' At their quizzical looks he explained about the time factor. 'If I can give Ward an approximate time those bullets were shot into Wilson's back — and it has to be after high noon — with a bit of work we can probably figure out where Alby was at that time, and who else was with him.'

Hood nodded and so did Stevens, who said, 'Glad I ain't goin' up agin that marshal.'

'A man to cultivate as a friend, I would think, rather than an enemy.' The doctor began to turn his horse. 'I'll just pass the information along to him and get on back home. There'll be patients getting ready to sleep on my porch by now if I don't.' He paused and reached inside his jacket. 'Oh, a messenger from Lucas McGill brought this out for you, Hood.'

He waved an envelope and Hood took it, looking more puzzled than ever.

They waved Hammond off and Hood tore open the envelope. He unfolded the single sheet of paper inside. He read the short message and snapped his head up, looking alarmed.

'Wh — what is it?' asked Stevens, concerned.

Then Hood grinned and handed him McGill's letter.

Stevens read quickly, looked, stared — and grinned.

'Well, you old son-of-a-gun! Hey, you're gonna be rich, Hood, ol' pard.'

'Pard's right. You and Trish are in this, too.'

'Aw, wait up, Hood, we — '

'Are my pardners in Anchor.' Hood tapped the letter. 'It's all in there, ain't it? The railroad spur around the wall was cancelled and now with that . . . ig . . . what was it? That kind of rock?'

'Igneous. The kind we tunnelled through for mines in Wyoming.'

'And some railroad engineer figures that instead of the spur track they can tunnel through it to this side of the

212

wall, and give 'em a downhill run all the way to Socorro. As it will cross my quarter-section, I'll — we'll — be paid compensation. Like you said, ol' pard, we'll be rich.'

Stevens seemed to have trouble coming to terms with it. 'If the railroad pays up. Ah, but McGill's honest as a parson, not that I know many parsons all that well. Yeah! Money for nothin'. I've heard it's possible.'

'Now we're gonna find out and . . . '

Stevens swallowed his next words as three fast rifle shots sounded from beyond the base of the rise where the trail passed around it, and where Doc Hammond had ridden only a few minutes ago.

★ ★ ★

Marshal Evan Ward heard the shooting, too, from where he was scouting for any clues that would help with Kelly's death.

He instinctively dropped a hand to

213

one of his guns as he spun around, hearing now the fast clatter of an approaching horse coming up the trail from around the bluff.

He glanced at his horse and the rifle still in the saddle scabbard, loosened it as a rider came in sight.

Ward identified him immediately.

Big Frank Cooper.

The rancher waved and veered across, skidding his sweating, exhilarated mount to a stop.

'Judas, Marshal, I knew you shouldn't've sent that sawbones after Hood! He's just shot Doc plumb outta the saddle!'

'What the hell're you talkin' about?'

'The doctor, for Chris'sakes! He come riding like the wind away from where Hood an' that Stevens feller were helpin' themselves to my mavericks, and he barely made it to the trail before Hood was after him, shootin' like a crazy man! Blew Doc clean off his mount, Marshal.'

'And what were you doin' over there?'

'Me?' Cooper blinked in surprise at

the question, but answered readily enough. 'Well, like I said, I figured it was a risky thing sendin' the sawbones over to ask Hood when he killed Wilson. He's smart enough to figure you were gettin' on to him, so I rode to warn Doc, but I was too late and . . . '

'I'll ask Hood myself,' cut in Ward. 'Here he comes. With Stevens, too.'

Frank fell silent; his horse, skittish and full of tension, was prancing about. By accident or design, it crashed into the lawman's mount and Ward swore as he fought to keep it on an even keel as it staggered and swerved precariously.

While his attention was diverted Frank Cooper rammed his mount again into the already off-balance horse and it went down, taking the marshal with it, rolling and kicking and squealing, pinning the lawman's right leg and bringing a mighty yell of pain from him.

Cooper triggered a couple of wild shots at Hood and Stevens and spurred away as they reined in their mounts to avoid crashing into the downed lawman.

Ward's horse was snorting and pawing the ground, heaving itself to its feet and bringing another cry of pain from Ward.

His right leg was a mangled mess, turned at an awkward and mighty painful angle. He thrashed in terrible agony, shouting: 'Git it offa me! Git the — goddam — jughead offa meeeeeeee!' not realizing that the animal had now run off, but his leg was mashed into the ground.

'Look after him, Steve,' Hood shouted, wheeling his horse aside and putting it after Cooper. 'I'll check on Doc.'

'Go!' Stevens yelled.

Ward snapped angrily: 'For Chris'sakes! You never mind Hood, mister. You tell me what the hell's goin' on — and now!'

Stevens nodded. 'Glad to, Marshal. Glad to.'

★   ★   ★

Hood managed to fire only two shots after the fleeing Cooper, then he spurred his already running mount back around the trail bend and reined up almost immediately.

Doc Hammond lay sprawled on the ground, his horse looking frightened as it stood at the edge of the timber, nostrils flaring, eyes rolling whitely.

Hood quit leather before his mount had stopped, ran stumblingly to where Doc Hammond lay, unmoving, his back a mess of fresh blood. Hood knew it was pointless feeling for a pulse, but he did so, anyway, and couldn't find one.

He sat back on his hams and took off his hat as he looked down at the medic's dead face.

'By God, the world's less of a place now you've gone from it, Doc. I can't bring you back, but I can make a little more room by getting rid of the bastard who did this to you. Rest easy, Doc, I doubt I'll ever meet the likes of you again. For which all of us are the poorer.'

Six-gun loads checked, rifle eased in the saddle scabbard so it could slide free without hindrance, Hood swung up into the saddle and spurred away towards the dust trail left hanging in the hot air by Frank Cooper's passing.

* * *

Trish was quite pleased with the first cake she had dared to bake in the new stove that Hood had bought — for the cabin, she reminded herself, not just for *her*!

But the gesture was there, and she felt a flush of joy because Hood had been so thoughtful. Steven had told her on the quiet that Hood had pledged money from the sale of his first lot of cattle to pay for it, and it had been a measure of the trust and goodwill the storekeeper in Hadleyville had felt for Hood that he had agreed.

He was indeed a thoughtful man with a big heart.

She heard a horse come into the rear yard, from the direction she was expecting Hood and Steven. With a small cry that was a mixture of pleasure and a little alarm, she hurriedly mopped her floury face with the apron before discarding it, and primped her hair swiftly as she made her way to the rear door.

Teeth flashing in a smile of welcome, she opened the door and gasped, stepping back hurriedly as a big, sweaty man used his bulk to force her back into the room. She opened her mouth to scream but a large, dirt-tasting hand clamped over her lips and a rough arm around her waist lifted her from the floor as she was carried bodily into the dim room.

Frank Cooper swept a passing glance over the sparsely furnished room and set her down with a thump that caused some of her hair to tumble across her face.

'Just do like you're told an' nothin'll happen to you. Gimme a hard time and I'll nail you by that hair to the damn door so your feet won't touch the ground. You savvy?'

He roared this last and she jumped, gulped, too frightened to speak, nodding vigorously. He flung her into a chair at the table, so violently that the chair overturned, taking Trish with it, skirts flying.

'Wh — what d'you want?' Trish stammered, and cringed when he rounded swiftly upon her, lifting and pinning her against the wall with big fingers encircling her slim throat.

'I want to kill Hood — and that stupid brother of yours if he gets in the way. I'll eventually kill you, too, but mebbe not right away. If you get my meanin'!'

She clawed at his eyes; it was a move he wasn't expecting and she was almost successful: her fingernails ripped a part of one eyebrow and the corner of the lid. He roared and instinctively clawed at his face, releasing her throat as he bit back a moan of pain.

'Yooouuu — *bitch!*' he choked, swaying, spittle flying as she spun away and lunged for the new stove.

Spare cast-iron stovetop lids were in a paper package on the end and she fumbled at these, ripping the paper wildly as Cooper recovered and, snarling like a demented animal, reached for her.

The package tore and she had the topmost lid in her hand, a small one about six inches in diameter and weighing a couple of pounds. She flung it in Frank's mad face as he grabbed at her. He got his head out of the way and as the lid clanged and bounced on the floorboards, she wrenched the next one out of the package. This one was about eight inches in diameter and pain shot through her slim wrist as she lifted and threw it. There was little force behind the throw and Frank swept it aside with a roar.

Frightened, Trish jumped back, slid away along the wall, dropping the rest of the package of heavy lids.

Frank roared in agony, holding his throbbing right foot, dancing what might have been seen as a humorous jig under other circumstances.

Funny or not — and it was definitely *not* as far as Cooper was concerned — Trish grabbed his shoulder as he bent over his near-broken foot, and pushed hard. He crashed against the stove, rolled halfway across the top. *Too bad the fire hadn't been lit!* He dropped off on to the floor, sobbing in pain.

Trish decided not to push her luck and ran for the door, slamming it behind her as she staggered away down the path past her gardens, sobbing to get a full breath into her lungs.

Reeling, she glanced behind her and saw him stumbling and leaping after her like a frog with a broken leg. Snarling, he threw himself at her.

She screamed and kicked, knowing there was no one to help her, as he crushed her back to the packed earth of the path. Her head hit hard and bright lights swirled and burst behind her eyes as she felt his huge weight crush her to the ground.

Hood knew there was only one place Cooper would make for.

Anchor.

The man was half-crazy at the best of times, with his raging inner spirit, but by now he must have blown part of his brain and gone about as crazy as any human could get.

His rage would include Trish, and Hood tried not to think about how he would treat her.

He clenched his fists as he jumped from the horse he had lashed and spurred recklessly through the timber, approaching his spread over the rise at the southern end of the wall. He was still a good half-mile from the cabin here but he moved on foot, rifle balanced in one hand, a Colt rammed into his waistband.

Fighting back all the images he was trying to avoid, he broke through a screen of brush. He looked down on to the rear of his cabin and saw the rear door swinging now from one hinge. He felt his gorge rise and threaten to choke him.

God! Cooper had already been here!

He knew what it meant, and he used massive willpower to blot out the fear for her safety that gripped him, knowing how small she really was, and how huge and powerful was Big Frank Cooper.

He almost dropped the rifle, his hand was sweating so much. Gripping it more firmly, his breathing ragged, he wasted breath on a curse: ragged breathing meant ragged, uncontrolled physical movements and thoughts. *Get a hold on yourself!*

He leaned against a tree, fought his immense impatience and made himself take twenty deep, steadying breaths. His brain cleared almost at once as large draughts of oxygen reached it, then he started down towards the cabin, noticing with surprise how quickly it was growing dark now.

There were no horses around but he

could see where the ground had been torn up by a racing mount skidding to a stop near that broken door. Through the opening, despite the dimness of the cabin's interior, he could see utensils lying on the floor, the table overturned.

He was crouched almost double as he slid along the wall right up to where the door hung on its single hinge. Then, gathering himself, he leapt through, rifle in both hands, butt rammed against his right hip, hammer cocked, finger on the trigger.

Nothing. Only the smell of spilled coffee, and some liquid that might have been a soup or the beginnings of a stew.

He was afraid to look in the bedroom, forced himself to do so, looking straight at the bed itself. He saw no young, despoiled body spread eagled to shock him. No . . .

But there was something.

A note, pinned to one crumpled pillow in a torn, soiled case. His hands shook as he spread it out, scraped a match into flame, found a stub of candle and lit it, set it on the window-sill.

Yeah, I've got her — the note read — *and I'm keeping her. If you want her, come and get her. But you get that close and you'll find her dead — and live just long enough to feel the misery of it before I kill you, too.*

* * *

Hood sagged back on to the bed, crumpling the note. Every filthy name he knew coursed through his mind and was directed at Frank Cooper. Uselessly, of course. All it proved was that he was human, and that was no great achievement at this moment.

He'll never give her back alive! He knows he's a dead man whatever he does — or doesn't do, now. So what's he got to lose?

Hood froze, hearing the thundering crack of his heart against his ribs. Startled, he found it hard to breathe as he heard — far off and faintly — her voice: 'Don't — worry — about me — Hood. Just kill this — snake!'

'You can bet on that, Trish!' he roared in answer.

He was shaking, mouth dry, then determination took over.

'You think you've got nothing to lose, Frank? Well, that works for me, too.'

His voice was cracking with the strain as he yelled his weak threat into the growing dusk.

A cold, answering laughter sent some homing birds wheeling and screeching.

'Frank? Here — I — come!'

The only answer was Trish's scream.

Hood ignored it. (*Tried to ignore it.*)

He couldn't completely, of course, but he made himself block it out as much as possible. He wasn't successful: he just wasn't that hard, but he managed to thrust the sound far enough back into his mind so that, while it registered, it was just *there*. Use it, you fool, he told himself. It's perfect as the driving force you need.

It drove him all right. He had always

been good at picking the direction of sounds at night. On more than one occasion he had saved his own life, and that of others with him, because he had chosen the right way to go, against all odds.

While he had been crouching here, gut-wrenchingly sick as he imagined Trish's suffering, his subconscious mind was setting him a direction, taking into account interfering echoes and rebound noises cutting through the gathering darkness.

It wasn't an easy path and he fell into a pit and thought he had broken a leg, he struck so hard. But, biting back sheer agony, he untangled his twisted limb and crawled out, lay there letting the pounding blood in his head settle until he could hear clearly again.

He moved off — at a right angle.

'Oh, Ho-ood! I hope you're still comin'. She ain't gonna last much longer.'

Neither are you, Hood murmured to himself, moving at an angle to the direction he had been heading.

Just keep talking, you sonuver. I'll find you. I'll — find — you.

Despite his injured leg he was moving quietly, old wartime habits coming back from their hiding-place in his subconscious. *Raider patrol! Strike fast, strike silent. Live to fight again.*

Just this once'll do this time, he allowed, and froze when Frank's voice came out of the darkness from only yards away: 'Where the hell are you, Hood? Mebbe I better have your gal give you a call, huh? But I warn you, it won't sound pretty.'

'And it won't *feel* pretty, Frank, when I get to you.'

Cooper actually gave a mild cry of surprise at the nearness of Hood's voice and he dropped flat. At the same time Hood heard the girl cry out: 'Hood! To your left.'

The last word was cut off with the sound of a slap, then Cooper fired his pistol, sweeping it in a tight arc as he blazed off six sweeping shots, hoping to find his target.

Hood dropped flat as soon as he heard the hammer cock and the lead tore and ripped through the undergrowth, covering his own movements as, instead of running or moving away from Cooper's position, he rolled towards it and was almost hit by Cooper's empty pistol as he dropped it and reached for a second Colt in his belt.

'*Hood!*' screamed Trish, distracting Cooper and earning another vicious slap for doing so.

Then Hood snapped erect and Cooper gave an almost hysterical cry as he discovered that Hood was much closer than he had estimated, so close their bodies were almost touching.

Frantically spinning aside, Frank tried to drag the girl closer, but she still had some fight left in her and kicked and kneed him. He twisted away, groaning, half bent over.

'Trish! Drop!' Hood yelled and he heard her gasp as he did so. He hoped it meant she had managed to fall to the ground.

Cooper got off one wild shot, the powderflash briefly showing Hood where Trish crouched on her knees — and Cooper stood, momentarily blinded by his own gun flash.

He jumped back, swinging the Colt around and shooting wildly. Trish screamed as another distraction and Hood saw Cooper snap his head around, quickly turning back and lifting his gun again. Hood stepped in, slammed his gun barrel across Cooper's wrist and heard the bone snap just seconds before he rammed his own gun barrel into Cooper's ribs.

'Time to say *adios*, Frank.'

He thumbed the hammer twice and Cooper was blown back against a tree, gagging as he dropped to his knees, gun rising pitifully slowly and weakly before he spread out on his face, blood gurgling into his throat.

Sobbing in near hysteria, Trish snatched Frank's gun and fired the last two shots into the dying body. The smoking weapon seemed to leap from her hands as she covered her face.

Then she was in Hood's arms and the tightness of her grip almost prevented him from breathing.

Almost — but not quite. He got his arms around her and held her very firmly.

'It's OK now, Trish. OK.'

'Yes! It *is*.' She fought to keep the sobs out of her voice but her face was wet against his.

He lifted a slightly shaking hand and used a thumb to brush the tears away.

'There'll be no more of those.'

And she knew he spoke the truth.

We do hope that you have enjoyed reading this large print book.

Did you know that all of our titles are available for purchase?

We publish a wide range of high quality large print books including:
Romances, Mysteries, Classics
General Fiction
Non Fiction and Westerns

Special interest titles available in large print are:
The Little Oxford Dictionary
Music Book, Song Book
Hymn Book, Service Book

Also available from us courtesy of Oxford University Press:
Young Readers' Dictionary
(large print edition)
Young Readers' Thesaurus
(large print edition)

For further information or a free brochure, please contact us at:
Ulverscroft Large Print Books Ltd.,
The Green, Bradgate Road, Anstey,
Leicester, LE7 7FU, England.
Tel: (00 44) 0116 236 4325
Fax: (00 44) 0116 234 0205

Other titles in the
Linford Western Library:

STAGECOACH TO WACO WELLS

Michael D. George

Trouble is coming, and it's due to arrive on the night train into Dodge City. Marshal Ben Carter has seen gunmen gathering at the railhead, waiting for their boss to return on the mighty locomotive speeding through the wilderness towards them. The marshal knows he is no match for the deadly men gathered like vultures. It seems like time to run or die — until bounty hunter Johnny Diamond arrives, and Carter proposes they join forces . . .